W9-BRR-985

Undead and Unappreciated

Berkley Sensation titles by MaryJanice Davidson

UNDEAD AND UNWED
UNDEAD AND UNEMPLOYED
UNDEAD AND UNAPPRECIATED

DERIK'S BANE

Undead and Unappreciated

MaryJanice Davidson

BERKLEY SENSATION, NEW YORK

THE BERKLEY PUBLISHING GROUP
Published by the Penguin Group
Penguin Group (USA) Inc.
375 Hudson Street, New York, New York 10014, USA
Penguin Group (Canada), 90 Eglinton Avenue East, Suite 700, Toronto, Ontario M4P 2Y3, Canada
(a division of Pearson Penguin Canada Inc.)
Penguin Books Ltd., 80 Strand, London WC2R 0RL, England
Penguin Group Ireland, 25 St. Stephen's Green, Dublin 2, Ireland (a division of Penguin Books Ltd.)
Penguin Group (Australia), 250 Camberwell Road, Camberwell, Victoria 3124, Australia
(a division of Pearson Australia Group Pty. Ltd.)
Penguin Books India Pvt. Ltd., 11 Community Centre, Panchsheel Park, New Delhi—110 017, India
Penguin Group (NZ), Cnr. Airborne and Rosedale Roads, Albany, Auckland 1310, New Zealand
(a division of Pearson New Zealand Ltd.)
Penguin Books (South Africa) (Pty.) Ltd., 24 Sturdee Avenue, Rosebank, Johannesburg 2196, South
Africa

Penguin Books Ltd., Registered Offices: 80 Strand, London WC2R 0RL, England

This book is an original publication of The Berkley Publishing Group.

This is a work of fiction. Names, characters, places, and incidents either are the product of the author's imagination or are used fictitiously, and any resemblance to actual persons, living or dead, business establishments, events, or locales is entirely coincidental. The publisher does not have any control over and does not assume any responsibility for author or third-party websites or their content.

Copyright © 2005 by MaryJanice Davidson Alongi.
Interior text design by Kristin del Rosario.

All rights reserved.
No part of this book may be reproduced, scanned, or distributed in any printed or electronic form without permission. Please do not participate in or encourage piracy of copyrighted materials in violation of the author's rights. Purchase only authorized editions.
BERKLEY SENSATION is an imprint of The Berkley Publishing Group.
BERKLEY SENSATION and the "B" design are trademarks belonging to Penguin Group (USA) Inc.

First edition: July 2005

Library of Congress Cataloging-in-Publication Data

Davidson, MaryJanice.
    Undead and unappreciated / MaryJanice Davidson.— 1st ed.
       p. cm.
    ISBN 0-425-20433-2
    1. Vampires—Fiction.   2. Nightclubs—Fiction.   3. Sisters—Fiction.   I. Title.

PS3604.A949U525 2005
813'.6—dc22

                                                                     2005043615

PRINTED IN THE UNITED STATES OF AMERICA

10   9   8   7   6   5   4   3   2   1

For my brother-in-law, Daniel,
who never complains.
No matter how often I try
to drag good gossip out of him, dammit.

Acknowledgments

This book would not have been possible without . . . me!

Also my husband, my PR person, my sister, my parents, my editor, my girlfriends, my agent, the copy editor, the cover artist, the sales reps, the marketing team, the booksellers, the makers of Godiva chocolates, and my readers.

But mostly me.

Author's Note

Of course, the devil's daughter doesn't really live in a suburb of Minneapolis. She lives in a suburb of Saint Paul. Duh.

Also, Betsy researched the Web for nondenominational wedding information and relied heavily on http://www.maggiedot.com/7Destiny/. Many thanks to the Reverend Marcia Ann George.

The Queene's sister shalt be Belov'd of the
Morning Star, and shalt take the Worlde.
—THE BOOK OF THE DEAD

Make a searching and fearless moral inventory of
yourself.
—ALCOHOLICS ANONYMOUS, STEP FOUR

Will you still need me, will you still please me,
when I'm sixty-four?
—JOHN LENNON AND PAUL McCARTNEY

Prologue 1: Secrets

Once upon a time, the devil was bored, and possessed a not-very-nice pregnant woman, and ran that woman's body for about a year.

The devil still drank and smoked, but only in moderation. The devil was good about taking prenatal pills but grumbled about the inevitable constipation.

And eventually, the devil gave birth to a baby girl.

After a month of diapers, night feedings, colic, laundry, spilled formula (the devil hated to breast-feed), and spit-up, the devil said, "Enough of this," and went back to Hell, which was infinitely preferable to living with a newborn.

The devil's daughter was adopted and grew up in a

suburb of Minneapolis, Minnesota. Her name was Laura, and she liked strawberry ice cream, and she never, ever missed church. She was a very nice young lady.

But she had a terrible temper.

Prologue 2: Problems

Thunderbird Motel
Bloomington, Minnesota
8:57 p.m.

"Okay, guys, let's set up here . . . Charley, you okay here? You got light?"

Her cameraman looked up. "It's shitty out here. Should be better inside."

"We won't film out here . . . we'll go inside the conference room. So, you're sure this is okay?"

The representative, who was smooth and sweatless like an egg, clasped his hands together and nodded slowly. Even his suit seemed to be free of threads or seams. "People need to see that it's not a bunch of chain-smoking losers who are afraid to go outside. There's doctors. There's lawyers. There's"—he stared at her with pale blue eyes, pilot's eyes— "anchorwomen."

Subtle, jerk. "Right, right. And we'll put all that across." She turned away from the AA rep, muttering under her breath. "Fuckin' slow news days . . . give me a war update anytime . . . okay! Let's get in there, Chuckles."

Charley knew his stuff, and with the new equipment, setup was not only a breeze, it was relatively quick and quiet. The conference room looked and smelled like a thousand others; sparse and scented of coffee. Interestingly, none of the room's inhabitants looked at them directly. There was a lot of coffee drinking and low chatting, a lot of nibbling on cheese and crackers, a lot of quiet milling and sideways glances.

They looked, the newswoman thought to herself, exactly like the man said. Respectable, settled. Sober. She was amazed they'd agreed to the cameras. Wasn't the second A supposed to be for *Anonymous*?

"Okay, everyone," the rep said, standing in the front of the room. "Let's get settled and get started. You all remember Channel 9 was coming tonight to help raise awareness . . . someone watching tonight might see we're not all villains in trench coats and maybe will come down."

"I'll start, and then we've got a new person here tonight . . ."

Someone the reporter couldn't see protested in a low yet
frantic voice, and was ignored—or wasn't heard—by the
rep. "I'm James," the rep continued, "and I've been sober
for six years, eight months, and nine days."

There was a pause as he stepped down, then a rustle, a
muffled, "Oof! Stupid steps." Then a young woman in her
mid-twenties was standing behind the small podium. She
squinted out at the audience for a moment, as if the fluo-
rescent lighting hurt her eyes, and then said in a completely mesmerizing voice, "Well, hi there. I'm Betsy. I
haven't had a drink in three days and four hours."

"Get on her!" the reporter hissed.

"I'm tight," Charley replied, dazzled.

The woman was tall—her head was just below the NO
SMOKING ON THESE PREMISES sign—which put her at
about six feet. She was dressed in a moss green suit with
the kind of suit jacket that buttoned up to her chin and
needed no underblouse. The richly colored clothing su-
perbly set off the delicate paleness of her skin and made
her green eyes seem huge and dark, like leaves in the middle of the forest. Her hair was golden blond, shoulder
length and wavy, with lovely red and gold highlights that
framed her face. Her cheekbones were sharp planes in an
interesting, even arresting face.

Her teeth were very white and flashed while she spoke.

"Okay, um, like I said, I'm Betsy. And I thought I'd come here . . . I mean, I saw on the Web that . . . anyway, I thought maybe you guys would have some tricks or something I could use to stop drinking."

Dead silence. The reporter noticed the audience was as rapt as Charley was. What presence! What clothes! What . . . Were those Bruno Maglis? The reporter edged closer. They were! What did this woman do for a living? She herself had paid almost three hundred bucks for the pair in her closet.

"It's just . . . always there. I wake up, and it's all I think about. I go to bed, I'm still thinking about it."

Everyone was nodding. Even Charley was nodding, making the camera wobble.

"It just . . . takes over. Totally takes over your life. You start to plan events around how you can drink. Like, if I have breakfast *here* with my friend, I can hit an alley afterward *there,* while she's going uptown. Or, if I blow another friend off for supper, I can reschedule on *him* and get my fix instead."

Everyone was nodding harder. A few of the men appeared to have tears in their eyes! Charley, thankfully, had stopped nodding, but was getting in on the woman as tightly as he could.

"Get the suit in the shot," the reporter whispered.

"I'm not used to this," the woman continued. "I mean, I'm used to wanting things, but not like *this*. I mean, gross."

A ripple of laughter.

"I've tried to stop, but I just made myself sick. And I've talked to some of my friends about it, but they think I should just suck it up. Ha-ha. And my new friends don't see it as a problem at all. I guess they're, what do you call them, enablers." More nods all around. "So here I am. Someone with a problem. A *big* problem. And . . . I thought maybe coming here and talking about it would help. That's all." Silence, so she added, "That's really all."

Spontaneous, almost savage, applause. The reporter had Charley pan back, getting the crowd's reaction. She wasn't sure the rep would let all their faces be shown on the ten o'clock news, but she wanted the film in the can, just in case.

She wanted Charley to get the woman walking to the back of the room, but when he panned back, she was gone.

The reporter and her cameraman looked for the gorgeous stranger for ten minutes, with zero luck. Neither of them could figure out how a woman could just disappear out of a small conference room.

Gone.

Shit.

Chapter 1

I took another slurp of my tea (orange pekoe, six sugars) and stuck out my left foot. Yep, last season's Brunos still looked great. Hell, they could be from the last decade and still look great. Quality costs . . . and it lasts, too.

Marc Spangler, one of my roommates, slouched into the kitchen, yawning. I withdrew my leg before he tripped and brained himself on the microwave. He looked like pan-fried hell, which was to say, he looked like he just came off shift. Since moving in with an emergency ward physician, I've discovered that your average doc comes off shift grimier than your average garbageman.

I greeted him warmly. "Another hard afternoon saving lives and seducing the janitor?"

"Another hard night suckering poor slobs out of their precious lifeblood?"

"Yep," we both said.

He poured himself a glass of milk and sat down across from me. "You look like you need some toast," I prompted.

"Forget it. I'm not eating food so you can get off on it secondhand. 'Ooh, ooh, Marc, make sure you smear the butter allllll over the bread . . . now let me smell it . . . don't you want some sweet, sweet jelly with that?' I've gained seven pounds since I moved in, you cow."

"You should have more respect for the dead," I said solemnly, and we both cracked up.

"God, what a day," he said. His hair was growing in nicely (he'd gone through a head-shaving phase this past summer), so now he looked like a clean Brillo pad with friendly green eyes. I wished my eyes were like that, but mine were murky, like fridge mold. His were clear, like lagoon water.

"Death? Bloodletting? Gang war?" Unlikely in Minnesota, but he looked pretty whipped.

"No, the fucking administration changed all the forms again." He rubbed his eyebrows. "Every time they do it, there's a six-month learning curve. Then when we've figured out who has to sign what and in what order, they change them again. You know, in the name of efficiency."

"That blows," I said sympathetically.

"What about you, what'd you do? Chomp on any would-be rapists? Or was tonight one of the nights you didn't bother to get anything to eat?"

"The second one. Oh, and I crashed an AA meeting."

He was halfway to the fridge for a milk refill and froze like I'd yelled "I see a Republican!" "You did what?"

"Crashed an AA meeting. Did you know they film those now?"

"They *what*?"

"I was kind of nervous because I didn't know if I'd have to, y'know, prove I was a drunk or if they'd take my word for it, or if I needed a note from a doctor or bartender or something, and it was kind of weird with the camera lights and all—"

He was giving me the strangest look. Usually I got that look from Sinclair. "It doesn't work like that."

"Yeah, I know, I found out. Really nice bunch of people. Kind of jumpy, but very friendly. Had to dodge the reporter, though."

"Reporter—" He shook his head. "But Betsy . . . why did you go?"

"Isn't it obvious?" I asked, a little irritably. Marc was usually sharper than this. "I drink blood."

"And did it work?" he asked with exaggerated concern.

"No, dimwad, it did not. The reporter and the lights

freaked me out, so I left early. But I might go back." I took another gulp of tea. Needed more sugar. I dumped some in and added, "Yep, I just might. Maybe they don't teach you the trick until you've gone a few times."

"It's not a secret handshake, honey." He laughed, but not like he thought what I'd said was funny. "But you could try that, see how that works."

"What's your damage? Maybe *you* should have a drink," I joked.

"I'm a recovering alcoholic."

"Oh, you are not."

"Betsy. I am."

"Nuh-uh!"

"Uh-huh."

I fought down escalating panic. Sure, I hadn't known Marc as long as I'd known, say, Jessica, but still. You'd think he would have brought something like that up. Or—ugh!—maybe he had, and I'd been so obsessed with the events of the past six months I hadn't—

"Don't worry," he said, reading my aghast expression and interpreting it correctly. "I never told you before."

"Well, I . . . I guess I should have noticed." I could put away a case of plum wine a month, and Jessica liked her daiquiris, and Sinclair went through grasshoppers like there was gonna be a crème de menthe embargo (for a studly vampire king, he drank like a girl), but I'd never noticed how Marc always stuck to milk. Or juice. Or water.

Of course, I'd had other things on my mind. Especially lately. But I was still embarrassed. Some friend! Didn't even realize my own roommate had a drinking problem. "I guess I should have noticed," I said again. "I'm sorry."

"I guess I should have told you. But there didn't ever seem to be a good time to bring it up. I mean, first there was the whole thing with Nostro, and then all the vampires getting killed, and then Sinclair moved in . . ."

"Ugh, don't remind me. But . . . you're so young. How did you even know you *were* one, much less decided to stop drinking?"

"I'm not *that* young, Betsy. You're only four years older than me."

I ignored that. "Is that why you were going to jump off the hospital roof when I met you?" I asked excitedly. "The booze had driven you to suicide?"

"No, paperwork and never getting laid had driven me to suicide. The booze just made me sleepy. In fact, that was the whole problem. Sleep."

"Yeah?"

"Yeah. See, being a med student isn't so bad. The work isn't intellectually hard or anything—"

"Spoken like a math genius."

"No, it's really not," he insisted. "There's just a lot of stuff to memorize. And they—hospitals—can't work a student to death. But they can work the interns and residents to death. And the thing is, when you're an intern, you're always short on sleep rations."

I nodded. I'd faithfully watched every episode of *ER* until they killed off Mark Green and the show started severely sucking.

"So it was normal to go forty, fifty hours sometimes without sleep."

"Yeah, but don't patients suffer because of it? I mean, tired people fuck up. Even someone who didn't go to Harvard Medical School knows that."

Marc nodded. "Sure. And it's not news to administration, either, or the chief residents, or the nurses. But the fuckups are blamed because a babydoc—that's what the interns are called—did it, not because he did it because he hadn't slept in two nights."

"Bogus."

"Tell me. They're supposed to limit the amount of hours you work, but it's not enforced. After a while you get used to it. You can't really remember a time when you weren't dog-ass tired. It starts getting hard to sleep even on your nights off. You're so used to being awake, and even if you do fall asleep, you know a nurse is going to wake you up in five minutes to handle a code or an admit, so why bother going down in the first place, and you just . . . stay awake. All the time."

He went back to the fridge, refilled his milk, took a sip, sat back down. "So, after a while I started having a few shots of Dewar's to help me get to sleep. A while after that, I started thinking on shift how great that shot of Dewar's would taste when I got home. A while after *that,* I started drinking whether I needed to get to sleep or not. And after that, I started to bring my old friend Dewar's to work."

"You drank . . . at work?" *And you drink blood,* I reminded myself. *Let's not start pointing fingers.*

"Yup. And the funny thing was, I remember the exact day I figured out I had a problem. It wasn't all the empty bottles I was recycling every week. It wasn't even the nipping at work or showing up at the EW with a hangover almost every day.

"It was this day I was working in Boston when I was asked to work a double, and I realized by the time I got off, all the bars and liquor stores would be closed. And I only had half a bottle of Dewar's at home. So I started calling around—to a bunch of my friends to see if one of them would run out and pick up a couple of bottles for me.

"And none of them would do it. Understandable. When

a pal calls you up practically in the middle of the night because he's desperate for his fix, you're not gonna help him, right? But the weird thing was, I was calling these people at eleven thirty at night, and none of them thought it was weird. That's when I knew."

"So what happened?"

"Nothing dramatic. Nobody died or anything. Nobody who wouldn't have, even if I'd been Marcus Welby and stone-cold sober. I just . . . stopped. Went home—"

"Dumped out the half bottle."

"Nope, I saved it. It was . . . like a charm, I guess. As long as the half bottle was there, I could fool myself into thinking I'd have a drink later. That was my trick. 'I won't have anything tonight, and tomorrow I'll reward myself with a big drink.' And of course, tomorrow I'd say the same thing. And I'm two years sober next month."

"That's . . ." What? Weird? Cool? Fascinating? "That's really an interesting story."

"Yeah, I can see the tears in your eyes. Which one did you go to?"

"What?"

"Which AA meeting?"

"Oh. Uh . . . the one at the Thunderbird Motel. On 494?"

"You should go to the one at the Bloomington Libe. Better stuff to drink."

"Thanks for the tip."

He drained his milk, gave me a milk-mustache smile, and slouched off toward his bedroom.

I drank cup after cup of tea and thought about Dewar's.

Chapter 2

Eric Sinclair, king of the vampires, was back from Europe the next night, I was sorry to see. It had been a relatively uneventful six weeks despite—or because of—the vampire king's voyage to Europe. I had been careful not to ask questions, because I didn't want him to misconstrue my interest in his activities as interest in him. On the top of my brain I figured he might be abroad to check on his holdings—they were on the vast side. On the bottom, I just didn't want to know.

"Welcome back," I said to Tina, his sidekick and oldest friend. Really old . . . like, two hundred years or whatever. "Die," I told him.

"I did that already," he replied, folding the newspaper

and setting it aside. "And I have no plans to do it again, not even for you, darling."

"I'll see you later, Majesties." Tina bowed and walked past us, out the room.

"Hi and 'bye," I said. "Why can't you follow her example?"

"Miss me?"

"Not hardly." This was sort of a lie. Eric Sinclair, at six foot huge, was an imposing presence. It wasn't just that he was big (broad shoulders, long legs) or great-looking (black eyes, dark brown hair, succulent mouth, big hands). He was charismatic . . . almost mesmerizing. You looked at him, and you wondered what it would be like to feel his mouth on you in the dark. He was sin in a suit.

"Come and sit down," Jessica said. "We're having a late supper. Really late."

"Jess." I sat. "How many times do I have to say this? You don't have to adjust your mealtimes just because the three of us sleep during the day."

"It's no big deal," she replied, which was a huge lie, since it was three o'clock in the morning, and she was finally having supper. Or a really early breakfast.

"You're so full of it." I poured myself a cup from the ancient tea service that had come with the house. Like just about everything in the place, it was a zillion years old and worth about that many dollars. I was almost getting used to using antiques every day. At least my heart didn't stop if I dropped something.

"I missed you," Sinclair said, as if I'd been having a conversation with him. "In fact, I was most anxious to return to your side."

"Don't start," I warned.

"No, start," Jessica said, slicing her roast beef. The smell was driving me crazy. Oooh, beef! I barely knew ye. "It's been creepily quiet around here lately."

"And I think it's time we addressed our current . . . difficulty."

"It is?"

He meant the fact that we were king and queen together, technically husband and wife, though we'd only had sex twice in the last six months.

"You can't turn back the clock, Elizabeth. Even one such as you has to bow to logic."

"Don't be a putz," I told him. "Pass the cream."

"I'm merely pointing out," he said, ignoring my request—both of them, come to think of it—"that you cannot be a little bit pregnant or go back to being a virgin. As we've already been intimate, and are married by vampire law—"

"Yawn," I said.

21

"—it's pointless not to share a room, and a bed."

"Forget it, pal." I got up and got the fucking cream myself. "Do I have to recap?"

"No," Sinclair said.

"But you will," Jessica added, not looking up from buttering her green beans.

"I slept with you once, and got stuck with the queen gig. Slept with you again, and Jessica invited you to move in."

"So, by that logic, I should give up intimate relations with Jessica," Sinclair pointed out, "not you."

"What kind of logic is that?" Jessica asked, almost laughing. "And you can just dream on, white boy."

"All of you, shut up and die."

"What'd *I* do?" she cried.

"You know what you did." I gave her a good glare, but she knew me too well and wasn't impressed. I decided to change the subject before we got into a real fight. Everybody knew my views on the subject. They had to be as tired of hearing about it as I was of bitching about it. "Where's Tina off to?"

"Visiting friends."

"I thought that's why you guys went to Europe."

"It's one of the reasons." Sinclair sipped his wine. "Marc is working, I assume?"

"You assume right. For once," I added, just in case it went to his head. His pointy head.

He ignored that, like he ignored 90 percent of what came out of my mouth. "I brought you something."

I was instantly distracted. And mad at myself for being distracted. And wildly curious . . . a present! From Europe! Gucci? Prada? Fendi?

"Oh, yeah?" I asked casually, but I nearly spilled hot tea all over myself, my hands started shaking so bad. Armani? Versace? "What'd you bring me, soap?" I tried to squash my soaring hopes. "It's soap, isn't it?"

He took a small, soap-sized black box out of his pocket and slid it over to me. I wasn't sure whether to be dismayed or excited. Small box = not shoes. But it could mean jewelry, which I liked as much as the next dead girl.

I flipped it open . . . and almost laughed. Strung on a silver chain—no, wait, it was Sinclair, and he never did anything halfway, so it was probably platinum—was a tiny platinum shoe, decorated with an emerald, a ruby, and a sapphire. The stones were so tiny they looked like a buckle on the shoe. It was just too adorable. And probably cost a fortune.

"Thanks, Sinclair, but I really couldn't." I slapped the box closed. I had drawn a line in the sand a few months ago, and it was tough work, sometimes, staying on my side of the line.

If I let him give me presents, what next? Sleeping together? Ruling together? Rewarding him for being sneaky?

Turning my back on my old life and forging through the next thousand years as the queen of the vampires? Lame. And again: lame.

"Keep it," he said mildly enough, but was that a flash of disappointment in his eyes? Or was it wishful thinking on my part? And if it was, what was the matter with me? "You might change your mind."

"If you ever come to your senses," Jessica mumbled to her green beans.

The thick, awkward silence was broken when Marc walked into the dining room. "Great, I'm starving. Is there any more beef?"

"Tons," I replied. "You're home early."

"Deader than hell at work, so I got off early. By the way, you've got visitors."

"Someone's here?" I put my hand on the necklace box . . . then took it away. What was I going to do with it? I didn't have pockets. Just hold it in my hand? Sinclair wouldn't take it back. Maybe leave it on the table? No, that'd be kind of bitchy. Right? Shit.

Why did he have to do this stuff? He must have known I wouldn't have accepted it. Right? Shit. "I didn't hear the doorbell." Stick it down the back of my pants and smuggle it out of the room? Hide it in my bra?

"I caught them on the porch. It's Andrea and Daniel. They said they need to ask you something."

24

I stood up, glad for a chance to get away from Awkward Dining 101. "Well, let's go see what they want."

"Don't forget your necklace," Jessica said brightly, and I almost groaned.

Chapter 3

Andrea Mercer and Daniel Harris were waiting for me in one of the parlors, and I was glad to see them. Not just because of the distraction. I really liked them.

Andrea was a vampire, like me, and a young one, also like me. She'd been killed on her twenty-first birthday, about six years ago, and was starting to get a handle on the thirst.

Daniel was her boyfriend, a regular guy and an outrageous flirt, and I got a real kick out of spending time with them. They were total opposites: she was serious and moody, and he was fun and irreverent. But you could tell they really loved each other. I thought that was pretty cool.

"Your Majesty," Andrea said, standing the minute she saw me. I waved her back down and sat down myself.

Daniel yawned and sprawled on the settee. He was a tall, blue-eyed, good-looking blond with the shoulders of a quarterback . . . put him in a horned helmet, and he'd be the spitting image of a marauding viking. He didn't stand when I entered, which was refreshing. "Betsy, babe. You guys can't have meetings at a decent hour?"

"Bitch, bitch, bitch," I said good-naturedly. "What's up, you guys?"

"Thanks for seeing us," Andrea said.

"No, thank *you*," I mumbled. If not for them I'd still be smiling awkwardly at Sinclair and trying to figure out where to stuff the necklace.

"We'll get right to it, ma'am. Daniel asked me to marry him."

"What? Seriously? That's great! Congratulations!"

"Thanks." Andrea smiled and looked at the floor, then back up at me. "And the thing is, we'd like you to do it."

"Do what?" Get married? According to some, I already was married.

But not according to me. As happy as I was for Andrea, I was suddenly so jealous I was ready to spit on her Payless-clad toes. Why, why, *why* couldn't Sinclair have *asked* me to marry him? Why did he have to trick me? Why did he bring me presents instead of apologizing and trying to make things right? If he loved me, he had a crummy way of showing it. And if he didn't, why did he fix it so we were stuck together for the next thousand years?

"To marry us," Andrea was saying. Oops, better pay attention. "To perform the ceremony."

"Oh." This was a new one. As the queen, I could do all sorts of things other vampires couldn't do. Handle crosses, drink holy water, accessorize. But perform vampire wedding ceremonies? "Uh . . . I'm flattered but . . . can I do that?"

"Yes," Sinclair said from two feet behind me. I nearly fell off the couch. The guy couldn't make noise when he walked like anybody else, oh no. Six foot four and as noisy as a cotton ball. "As the sovereign, you can perform any ceremony you wish, including weddings."

"Oh. Jeez, you guys, I don't know what to say . . ."

"Say yes," Daniel said. "Because we can't get a priest. And Andy's got her heart set on you doing it, don't ask me why."

Andy (not that anybody else could get away with calling her that) nodded. "That's true."

"Which part?" I teased.

"All of it. Will you help us?"

"But . . ." But I didn't know how. But I wouldn't know what to say. But it would be really depressing for me to marry another couple, knowing I would never have a proper wedding. But it was ridiculous, having a secretary perform the wedding ceremony. "When's the big day?" I asked, surrendering.

They looked at each other, then back at me. "We figured we'd leave that up to you," Daniel said. "You know, with your busy queen schedule and all." Typical guy.

"When do you want to get married?" I asked her. She'd have picked out a date the second he proposed.

She hesitated for a second, glanced at Daniel, then said, "Halloween."

"Oh, cool!" And it would be. *So* cool. A Halloween wedding ceremony . . . with vampires! Plus, more than two weeks to figure out exactly what the heck I was supposed to do.

Daniel looked vaguely alarmed. Again, typical guy. "That's kind of quick, don't you think?"

"That's okay," I said, trying to catch Andrea's eye while she glared daggers at her beloved. "Yeah, okay, that'll work. Do you want to have it here?"

Again she hesitated, and again she glanced at Daniel, who shrugged and relaxed back on the couch. "If that wouldn't be too big an imposition, Your Majesty."

"It's no trouble. It's not like we don't have the space. Besides, we haven't had a decent party here in . . . ever." I started to cheer up a little, picturing myself in a severe black suit and pumps in maybe a dark purple. Or burnt orange, for the holiday? No, purple.

"Thank you so much," Andrea was saying—oops, they were leaving. All business, that was Andrea. Plus Daniel was still yawning. It couldn't be easy, adjusting to the undead's schedule. I used to waitress at a truck stop during graveyard shift (years before I knew what the graveyard shift *really* was), and no matter how much I slept during the day, I always wanted a nap around four a.m. "We'll be in touch."

"No problem," I replied, walking them to one of the house's sixty doors. "Talk to you soon. And congratulations again."

They said their good-byes, the door shut, and I turned to see Sinclair had followed me. "He asked her to marry him?" he asked, staring after them thoughtfully.

"Yeah," I replied. "You should try it sometime." Then I walked past him and marched up the stairs to my bedroom.

Chapter 4

Which was really stupid, because I had work to do tonight. I had to check on Scratch and the Fiends. So I pushed up my bedroom window, popped the screen, stuck a leg over the windowsill, and jumped.

One of the few nice things about being dead is it's pretty much impossible to die again. So a three-story fall was no problem at all. It didn't hurt; it didn't even knock the breath (what breath?) out of me. It was like jumping off the bed.

I hit the grass, rolled, stood up, shook the dead leaves out of my hair, examined the grass stain on my left knee . . . then remembered I'd forgotten my keys and my purse, and went to ring the front doorbell.

Finally, I was in my car, headed to my nightclub, Scratch.

It wasn't really mine. Okay, it was, by vampire law, which was confusing. The way it worked was, if you kill a vampire, all their property becomes yours. Vampires generally don't have kids or families to leave stuff to, and probate only happens during daylight hours anyway. So, I'd killed this rotten vampire, Monique, and she owned, like, eight businesses, and now they were all mine, but the only one I was really interested in was Scratch. I had Jessica's accountant put all the others—the school, the French restaurant, the Swiss spa (that one hurt to let go)—up for sale. Tried to, anyway. It was complicated not least because I couldn't prove I legally owned them. And, like a stubborn ass, I didn't want Sinclair's help. If they sold, I'd worry about what to do with the money later. Meanwhile, I was trying to hang on to Scratch, but it wasn't easy.

I was glad Monique was gone—well, dead. And not because I got her car and her businesses. Not *just* because of that. Monique had been bad, even for a vampire. She'd tried—repeatedly—to kill me, but worse, she'd killed other vampires to get to me. And she'd ruined my shirt. She had to go.

I'd been a secretary and office manager for years before I died, so managing a nightclub—handling the paperwork, anyway—was something I could actually do. Probably. If the other vampires would give me a chance. Trouble was, they hated my guts. I guess employee loyalty was big in the vampire world. They were pretty pissed that I'd offed the boss.

Not that any of them told me that in so many words. No, they kept their gazes averted and didn't speak to me unless spoken to. This made it easy to give orders but tough to strike up a conversation.

So I pulled up outside the club—it looked like an old brownstone, except with valet parking—and went inside. Deader than shit (no pun intended), as usual.

"Okay, well," I told one of them . . . I was having the worst time remembering their names. Probably because they never volunteered them. And vampires didn't go for those blue and white HELLO MY NAME IS ——— stickers. "We've got to get customers to start coming here again."

"Your Majesty knows how to do that," he replied, staring over my shoulder, which always made me think there was a monster sneaking up on me. Maybe there was. He was about my height, and about my coloring—blond, with light eyes—long slender fingers, and (no joke!) a slight overbite.

"Don't start up with that shit," I told Slight Overbite. "I mean a way to get customers where eighty people don't die a week."

See, the way the vampires liked to run things, they could

have "sheep," a detestable word that meant a human slave/partner, and they could drink blood right out on the dance floor, and if a regular person got on their nerves, bye-bye regular person. Forget it! It was morally wrong, and I'd never get OSHA off my ass.

"That was under the old management," I told him. "We've been over this. Look, we can run a profitable nightclub for vampires without having to be horrible to regular people."

"We can?" he asked, now looking around at the totally deserted dance floor.

"Oh, shut up. Look: put your thinking cap on your tiny little head, because we're doing it. If you were a dead guy, wouldn't you like to hang out in a place where you won't get hassled?"

"Yes. And where I could drink and have fun."

"No, *no*. I mean, yeah, drink, have a daiquiri, have three, go crazy. Not . . . you know." I made a slashing gesture across my throat.

He shrugged.

"We're *going* to make it work, Slight Overbite," I reminded him. This had been my mantra for the last three months.

He shrugged again.

* * *

"Majesty!" Alice cried, running out to greet me. At least somebody was happy to see me tonight. Well, that wasn't fair. Andrea and Daniel had been happy to see me. They'd even *come* to see me. Well, to ask a favor. Still, it was nice to have any kind of company. "Welcome! You should have told me you were coming."

"How's it going, Alice?" As always, I admired her undead creamy complexion (she'd been turned into a vampire after puberty but before adolescence really got its claws into her, so no zits, ever). "How are the Fiends doing?"

"Really well," she enthused. "One of them escaped, but I got him back before he killed anyone this time."

I shuddered. "Good work. Is it the same one, the one who keeps getting out?" Nostro's property—another vampire I killed, and don't go making assumptions, because I'm not that kind of queen—had a high fence around it, but the Fiends were weirdly clever. More animal than human, they were vampires who hadn't been allowed to feed and had gone feral. This happened under previous management, you understand.

Anyway, I didn't feel right about staking them—it wasn't *their* fault they'd gone insane with a supernatural hunger for blood—and resisted heavy pressure from Sinclair and Tina to put an end to them. Alice was my Fiend keeper. She kept them clean, kept them fed, kept an eye on them, kept them from feasting on the local children.

"It's George," Alice confirmed. "He's a free spirit, I guess."

He was an insane nutty vampire who forgot how to walk upright, but never mind. "I can't believe you've named them. Sinclair freaked when you told him. Run them by me again."

"Happy, Skippy, Trippy, Sandy, Benny, Clara, Jane, and George."

I laughed. "Right, right. Good job." I tried to sober up. Poor things. It wasn't right to laugh at them. "So, you got George back?"

"Yes. He wasn't out for long this time. If you're looking for him, he's right behind you, Majesty."

I whirled. I loathed how vampires could sneak up on me, and the Fiends were . . . well, fiendish. George looked exactly like the others, with raggedy long hair, long filthy nails (Alice did her best, but like all of us, she had her limitations), unkempt and hungry-looking, with filthy clothes.

Though, thanks to Alice, they didn't look quite as wild-eyed as usual. They scuttled like dogs . . . she was trying to remind them how to walk upright, but they always toppled over, then scampered away. The others stuck around, since they were being fed, but George was a wanderer.

Right now, he was inching toward me and sniffing the air. The Fiends, luckily for me, were weirdly devoted. In fact, they'd devoured Nostro for me. (I tried to delegate when I could.)

"Quit that," I told him. I never knew how to speak to them. It was wrong to treat them like pets, but they weren't exactly human, either.

"Stop running away. Be good and listen to Alice."

"I don't exactly talk to them," she explained. "But I appreciate the support, Majesty."

"How's the house? Everything running okay?" I was talking about Nostro's sprawling mansion and grounds, which—have I mentioned this?—were all mine since I'd axed his sorry bloodsucking butt this past spring. You couldn't pay me to live in the creepy place, though, so Alice was my caretaker. Unlike *some* unnamed employees of a certain nightclub I could mention, she was helpful and nice. "You'd tell me if you needed a hand, right?"

"Oh, yes, Majesty," she lied. It was a point of pride with Alice that I relied on her so heavily to take care of the Fiends for me. She'd never admit to needing help. Yes, George got out once in a while, but if not for her, they'd *all* be out, all the time.

Sure, I felt bad about the two guys he'd eaten, but since the guys in question had been devoured while attacking lone women on the street, not *too* bad. "Of course, I would let you know. But everything's fine." She looked down at George, who was nibbling on his palm and looking up at the moon. "We're all fine."

Chapter 5

I stared at the baby shower invitation. It was pink (yur-rggh), and sparkly, and seven inches high (how did she find envelopes to fit?) and in the shape of a baby carriage.

Come and celebrate!
Antonia's having a baby!
(Baby registry at Marshall Field's,
612-892-3212, please no green or purple)
4:00 p.m., October 7th

"Bitch," Jessica commented, reading over my shoulder. "She's having it during the day, when you can't come."

"Not that I'd want to," I sniffed, but the fact was, the baby-to-be was my half sibling, poor thing.

"Whatcha gonna get her?"

"The Ant? How about a brain aneurysm?"

Jessica walked past me and opened the fridge. "You have to get her something. I mean, the baby something."

"How about a new mother?"

"She's registered, anyway."

"Not *too* gauche, putting it right on the invitation. With color preferences!"

"Yes, yes . . . how about a portacrib?"

"A what?"

"It's a crib that folds up and you can take it around."

"Why," I demanded, gesturing for her to pour me a glass of milk as well, "would you want to take a crib around?"

"That way, if the baby comes to visit, it's got a place to sleep."

"You think the baby will make a break for it so soon?" I answered my own question. "Of course it will. Poor thing will probably sneak right out of the hospital nursery."

"Will you be serious, please?"

"I can't. If I think about it seriously, my head will blow up. It's just one more awful thing in my life right now—physical proof that my father is still having sex with the Ant."

"It must be hard to take," she agreed, "on top of being dead and all."

"Tell me." I took a gulp of milk. Being dead, being Sinclair's consort, living in this museum-sized mausoleum, trying to run Scratch (it was the only money I had coming in), trying to keep the Fiends on a short leash (literally!), trying to make nice with Dad and the Ant, and finally . . . "So, check this. Andrea and Daniel are getting married."

"And you're performing the ceremony."

"How'd you know?"

"Sinclair told me."

"Look, I forbid you to speak with that man."

"I'm his landlord," she reminded me. "We were making polite conversation while he wrote out his rent check."

I snorted. Like she needed the money. Jessica was rich. Not "compared to the rest of the world everyone in America is rich" rich. *Rich* rich. Like, Bill Gates tried to get her to loan him money for a new start-up rich. She turned him down politely, via email. Said it was her way of evening up the universe.

"This whole thing is ridiculous, you know. It's ridiculous that we live in this place. It's ridiculous that *he* lives with us. It's ridiculous that you're charging him rent, and it's really ridiculous that he pays it. You two have all the money in the world, and you're just trading it back and forth."

"Like baseball cards," she suggested.

"It's not funny, Jessica."

"It's a little bit funny. Besides, what was I supposed to do? After Nostro burned down his house, he was living on hotel room service. And it's not like we didn't have the space."

I had nothing to say to that, just gulped more milk and slumped at one of the kitchen stools. The room was laid out like an industrial kitchen, except the whole second half had a big table with chairs, and there was a long counter that ran a fourth of the length of the room, also with chairs. It was by far the most inviting room in the house, which is why I usually hung out there. I just didn't feel right in one of the parlors or the library.

Besides, the Book of the Dead was in the library. Like last year's *Vogue*s weren't bad enough.

"Someone's at the door," I said, wiping off my face.

"Oh, there is not."

"Jessica, there totally is."

"No way. You know, you're like one of those annoying yappy little dogs . . . every time a car rolls by outside, you freak out and decide someone's coming up the walk and ringing the—"

Bonnnnnnng-BONNNNNNNNNNGGGGG.

"I hate you," she sighed, getting up.

I checked my watch. It was almost six o'clock in the

morning . . . probably not a vampire. They didn't like to be running around so close to sunrise. As a rule, they were more flammable than gasoline. Or was it inflammable? I always got those two mixed up. My D in chemistry had never served me well.

Sinclair walked in, winding his watch.

"You really need to get something battery-operated," I told him.

"My father gave this to me. And speaking of fathers . . ."

"Don't tell me." I covered my eyes. Should have covered my ears instead. "Don't even tell me."

"Guess who decided to stop by?" Jessica asked brightly, walking back into the kitchen. That was quick—she must have sprinted there and back.

I dropped my hands in time to see a tall, good-looking older man walking behind her, puffing to keep up, his dark brown hair heavily flecked with salt, the golfing pants tightly cinched at the waist with an alligator belt, the pink plaid complemented by the pink Izod shirt.

"Dad," I said with as much enthusiasm as I could muster, which wasn't a lot. He'd obviously stopped by en route to the links, which should have been touching, but wasn't.

"Betsy. Err . . ." He nodded at Sinclair, then his gaze skittered away. This was a pretty typical reaction when a guy met Sinclair. Women looked away, too . . . but always looked back.

"You look nice." I pointed to the corners of my eyes. "Get something done?"

His crow's feet had radically depleted, and he nodded. In fact, he looked better than he had in years. I was so happy my death wasn't, y'know, weighing heavily on him or anything. "Yes, your stepmother had me go see Dr. Ferrin. He does the mayor, too," he added, because he couldn't help himself.

Like Sinclair or Jessica cared . . . or needed it themselves. I looked at him but, as usual, Sinclair didn't take the hint. In fact, he was—oh, Lord!—sitting down at the table and making himself comfortable.

"I see you got the announcement," Dad said, glancing down at my mail, scattered across the counter. I'd always assumed being dead cut down on junk mail, but like so many things I'd assumed about death, I was wrong.

"Invitation," Jessica piped up, also sitting down. "Not announcement. Invitation."

"Well . . . but you can't come . . . because it's . . . you know . . ."

"I would be happy to go instead," Sinclair said with all the warmth of a rutting cobra. "In fact, it would be appropriate if I did. Why . . ." He grinned, which was horrifying, but also kind of funny. "I'm practically a member of your family."

I actually felt sorry for my dad; for a second I thought he was going to faint, just do a header into my mail pile. Sinclair, as an ancient dead guy, could walk around during the day, provided he stayed inside. Maybe he could borrow a fire blanket for going to and from the taxi.

A mental image of big-shouldered Sinclair in one of his sober suits, sitting primly on one of the Ant's over-stuffed couches, a pink ribboned gift in his lap . . . it was too much.

I was annoyed with the big goober, as usual, but it was kind of cute the way he stuck it to my dad on my behalf. Talk about the son-in-law from hell.

"You gonna be okay?" I asked Dad, fighting a grin. Jessica, I noticed, had given up that fight.

"I—I—I—"

"You could wear the black Gucci," Jessica told Sinclair. "I picked it up from the cleaner's yesterday, so it's all set to go."

"Kind of you, dear, but I have told you many times, you are not an errand runner."

"I—I—I—"

"I was there anyway, getting my own stuff." She shrugged. "No trouble."

"I—I—I—"

"You are too kind, Jessica."

"I—I—I—"

"It's all right, Dad," I said, forcing myself to pat his shoulder. "I won't let him come if you don't want him there."

"But I adore baby showers!" Sinclair protested, having the gall to sound wounded. "I find them scrumptious."

"I just . . ." My dad took a deep gulp of air and tried to steady himself. I stopped patting. "I just wanted to make sure you got the . . . the announcement. But I also wanted to remind you . . . your stepmother is very delicate . . . very . . . under a lot of stress, you know . . . the baby . . . and the spring carnival . . . she's chairwoman . . . and I don't think . . . don't think . . ."

"Stress." Jessica snorted. "Yeah, that's the problem. What's the shrink du jour say?"

"Dr. Brennan comes highly recommended," my father said and, because he couldn't help it, added, "He's very exclusive *and* expensive, but he made room on his calendar for Antonia. He feels she should avoid stress and . . . and unpleasantness."

"Maybe she should stop looking in the mirror," Jessica suggested, and I chewed on my lower lip, hard, so I wouldn't laugh. I had to admit, I was getting more yuks out of this predawn meeting than I'd had in about a month. Maybe it was a good thing Sinclair was back.

What was I thinking?

My father turned his back on Jess but said nothing. She was black, which meant he had a hard time taking her seriously: but she was also the richest woman in the state, so he couldn't afford to totally blow her off. It was a tricky balancing act, one he usually fucked up. "You understand what I'm saying, don't you, Betsy?" he almost pleaded.

"Sure. Send a gift, but don't visit."

Sinclair was on his feet, but my dad, who had his back to that part of the room, didn't notice. Poor survival skills—outside of the boardroom—that was my father. Jessica reached out and tugged, hard, on his jacket, but Sinclair didn't budge.

"It's okay," I added, waving Sinclair back down—but he still didn't budge, the stubborn tick. "I didn't want to go, anyway."

Dad relaxed and smiled at me. "Well, of course, that's what I assumed."

"Of course." I gave him a wintry smile in return, which, I was glad to see, backed him up a step. "Thanks so much for stopping by. My love to what's-her-name."

"Betsy, you've never understood Antonia—"

"I understand her fine."

"No, I don't think someone like you could ever understand—"

"Mr. Taylor!" We all jumped. The crockery had practically rattled. And my dad had nearly swooned again. "I demand you retract that statement *at once,* or I will be forced to—what are you doing?"

Jessica had jumped on Sinclair's back in an attempt to forestall the lecture (or possibly the maiming). She was clinging to him like a skinny black beetle, all arms and elbows and knees, and he shook his head, which nearly dislodged her. "Really, Jessica. Could you climb down?"

"Promise you won't finish that sentence," she whispered in his ear. "Take it from me. It won't do any good, and it might make things worse. She can handle him."

Anybody else would have said something like, "Hello, I'm standing right here!" but my dad, the master of ignoring what was in his face, didn't say a word. He brushed a piece of lint off his shirtsleeve and examined his Kenneth Coles, which were glossy with shoeshine, while my best friend climbed my consort like a premenstrual monkey.

"I certainly will not. She is my consort and my queen, and he is treating her like—"

"So," my dad interrupted, cutting Sinclair off, which nobody ever got away with except me, "I'll tell Antonia you said hi."

"Why?" I asked, honestly curious.

You have to understand, it's not like my dad was incredibly brave or anything. He had a pissed-off billionaire and a vampire king in the room, but it didn't phase him, because it was beneath him. He could just close his mind to anything remotely unpleasant—or even interesting. I'd gotten used to my father's oblivious ways by the time I was thirteen, when I realized he'd tossed my mom, and the Ant was going to be my stepmother. Since he was the only dad I had, I put up with a lot. But, to be fair, so did he.

"It won't be like the last time," my dad continued, sounding almost cheerful. "She was all alone last time, but this time I'm here, and she'll have all the support she needs. I just wish you could understand what she's been through, how hard she . . . she . . ." He trailed off as I stared at him, as he realized he'd just made a fuckup of truly heroic proportions.

"She's been pregnant before?" I asked, almost gasped.

Jessica *did* gasp. "Get out of town!"

"No—no, she didn't . . . I mean, I wasn't—she wasn't—we—we—"

"Was there a baby?" Sinclair asked quietly, and good as he was, my dad couldn't ignore that and turned around to face him, moving stiffly like a puppet whose strings were being jerked. Which probably wasn't that far from the truth.

"Yes."

"And"—Sinclair took a step closer (Jessica was still hanging on to his back, gaping over his shoulder at my dad) and looked down at my father—"were you the father?"

"Yessss." My dad sounded drugged. But then, anybody did once Sinclair got close enough. He was the best I'd seen at it. I could only entrance men, but he could do anybody.

"Where is the baby?"

"Antonia didn't tell me . . . didn't . . . we weren't together, and she gave it . . . she didn't . . . she . . ."

"You better stop," I said. "He's about to blow all his cylinders."

"Quite right," Sinclair said. "That would be truly terrible."

I gave Sinclair a look, then took my dad by the shoulders. "Dad. Dad! Listen. You came over and made sure I wasn't going to come to the shower."

"Yes, I made sure of that," he agreed, focusing on me at once. "Antonia insisted."

I gritted my teeth. *Bitch!* "But I didn't want to go anyway, so it all worked out fine."

"Yes, you refused to go, so it really was all for the best."

"And I looked like hell."

"Yes, you looked terrible, being dead isn't agreeing with you at all, not at all, just like Antonia said it wouldn't."

"Now go golfing and," I added spitefully, "stroke three figures."

"Ouch," Jessica said as my father marched out.

"I am just not believing this," I said, massaging my temples. "Like I don't have enough to worry about. I can't believe he let that slip."

"You have that effect on men," Sinclair said kindly. "They always reveal more than planned to you."

I shrugged but was inwardly pleased. "How long has he been carrying this secret around? Why did he just happen to blurt it out while you and I were in the room? Jessica, would you climb down, for heaven's sake? I'm dying to know the rest. I mean, I might have a brother or sister running around *now*."

"This doesn't bode well for your stress levels," Jessica commented, letting go of Sinclair's neck and dropping to the floor.

"We will find out more. Your father has incomplete information anyway. We should go directly to the source."

"Antonia," Jessica and I said at the same time.

Chapter 6

Sinclair's convertible was ridiculously crowded. He was driving, I was riding shotgun (finally, a perk to our "relationship"), and Marc, Jessica, and Tina were in the backseat.

Tina had come because . . . well, she always came with Sinclair when we were doing vampire stuff. The two of them went way back—in fact, she'd turned him. She was like his combination best pal/secretary/enforcer/confidant. Which was fine with me, because I sure as shit didn't want to do any of those things.

We had decided Marc should come along because we planned to drag all the gory details out of the Ant, and you never knew when a physician might come in handy.

Jessica, however, had blackmailed her way along. Sinclair had a lot of odious qualities, I'll be the first to say it (again and again); but one thing he liked to do was keep my friends out of vampire issues. And I couldn't really blame him . . . you just never knew when a totally normal vampire errand would end in a bloodbath with severed-limb soap.

Jessica never accepted these excuses. She put her size-nine foot down and that was the end of it. The clincher was when she told Sinclair it would be a shame if anything happened to any of his European suits while they were at the dry cleaners.

"In the old days," he'd replied, "errand runners were actually helpful." But that was all he'd said about it; Sinclair was always impeccably dressed, and had all his stuff tailor made. It wasn't being rich and wanting the best; his shoulders were too broad and his waist too narrow to buy off the rack. I could only imagine what his clothes cost. I had the feeling he would have let Jess ride in the passenger seat if she'd threatened his best Gucci.

So it was crowded, but almost nice. If it weren't for where we were going.

"It's just a word," Marc was insisting. Oh, not this again. Jessica hated "African American," but she wasn't too crazy about the N word, either. "It's lost all meaning. This isn't the nineteenth century. Or even the twentieth."

"I don't think we should be talking about this," Tina

said, shifting so Marc's elbow wasn't on her eyebrow. She was teeny, but it was a tight fit back there.

"No, it's fine," Jessica replied.

"Of course it's fine, we're all civilized ad—well, we're all adults. Tina, I swear, you're the most politically correct dead person I've ever known."

"I just don't think this is an appropriate discussion for—for us." Tina had been born around the time Lincoln freed the slaves, so she had perspective the rest of us didn't. She was pretty closemouthed about the whole thing.

"No, no, no," Jessica said, and I curled my fingers around the door handle, just in case. I knew that tone. "In this day and age, there are quite a few more important things to worry about. It *is* just a word. It's totally lost its meaning." Sinclair was looking up at her in the rearview, and Tina was edging away. Only Marc, who couldn't smell emotions, was oblivious. "Now go ahead," she continued calmly. "You just call me that *once*."

Silence. Followed by Marc's meek, "I didn't mean we should go around calling other people that. I just think— I mean I don't think—not that anyone should call you—or call anyone—"

"Will you stop already before one of us has to knock you unconscious?" I asked.

Jessica snickered, and that was the end of the discussion for that week.

* * *

We pulled upside my dad's Tudor (four thousand square feet for two people!) and piled out of the car. It was full dark, about nine o'clock at night. My dad had left town that afternoon for a business trip, and the Ant would be alone.

This information was helpfully provided by my mother, who supported my vampiric pursuits and helped me out whenever she could. Sometimes it's like that, I've noticed . . . one parent is almost too great, and the other one's a shit. I had my mom so high up on a pedestal, the poor thing probably got oxygen deprived.

I rapped twice, then opened the front door. Unlocked, of course . . . it was a pretty nice neighborhood. Very low crime. My dad didn't even lock his BMW when he left it in the driveway. As far as I knew, they'd never been robbed. Of course, if my funds ever ran low, that might change.

"Helloooooo?" I called. "Antonia? It's me, your favorite stepdaughter."

"And by favorite," Marc added, stepping into the foyer behind me, "she means hated." He seemed to be bouncing back nicely from his humiliation in the car . . . but then, he was pretty irrepressible. Once you overlooked the whole attempted-suicide thing. Come to think of it, it was an *attempted* suicide . . .

58

"You haven't even met her," Jessica said as we all crowded into the small hall.

"No, but I've heard the legend. Frankly, I'm skeptical. Can she live up to the hype?"

"I have to admit," Tina said, "I'm curious, too."

"She knows you are a vampire, but the front door was unlocked." Sinclair sniffed. "Either she's unbelievably arrogant or unbelievably dim."

"You can't be here!" my stepmother said by way of greeting, running down the stairs like Scarlett O'Hara with a blond wig and frown lines. "I didn't invite you in!"

"That only works on black people," Jessica said.

Tina's eyes went wide, the way they do when she's concentrating on not laughing. "I'm afraid that's an old wives' tale, ma'am."

"Always a pleasure, Antonia," I said dryly. "Wow, you've gained a *ton* of weight."

She glared blondly. Her hair was the perfect color (and possibly texture, but I wasn't planning on touching it) of a cut pineapple. She had on more blue eye makeup than a seventies disco queen, and her lipstick was a shade redder than her lip liner. Nine o'clock at night, home alone, husband out of town, and in full makeup. And black miniskirt. And white silk blouse, sans bra. Unreal.

"You get out of here and take your friends with you," she said. She had been born and raised in Bemidji, but popped her consonants like she'd spent one too many years at an East Coast finishing school. "I told your father I don't know why he doesn't just wash his hands of you, and I'll tell you to your face. And another thing: I don't want you around the baby; I don't care if you're the big sister of the baby or not; you should have had the decency to stay dead like any normal person would stay dead."

"She *does* live up to the hype," Marc said, goggling at her.

"I couldn't agree with you more on that last one," I said. "This is Marc, my gay roommate." The Ant was, among other charming things, a homophobe. "And this is Sinclair and Tina." What they were was obvious. "We're here to ask you a few questions."

"Well, I'm not talking to you. I can't believe you had the nerve to even come here like a normal person when you're . . . you're . . ."

"A Republican?" I asked, possibly starting to enjoy this.

"We just have a couple of questions, and then we'll get right out of your hair," Jessica said. I could tell she was dying to say what she was about to say. "About the baby you *already* had."

The Ant, unfortunately, wasn't taken by surprise in the slightest, which meant my dad had warned her about his little slip. That was annoying. And surprising. My dad was pretty firmly under the Ant's manicured thumb. He lived in fear of her surgically plumped lips tightening in anger.

Instead, she took a breath and may have frowned, but she was fairly heavily Botoxed so it was hard to be sure. "You just mind your own business and get out of here, because it's nothing you need to worry about, and I can't believe you came all the way down here just to ask me about that. It's ancient history."

"All the way down here?" Marc asked. "You live in Edina, not darkest Africa."

"And are we going to stand in the foyer all night?" Jessica complained.

"I'm surprised we got this far," I replied.

"No, you're not staying in here all night. In fact, you're leaving right now." She dug around in her pocket and then whipped out a cross she had obviously made out of popsicle sticks. "The power of Christ compels you! The power of Christ compels you!"

I burst out laughing, even as Tina and Sinclair both took a big step back and looked away.

"I *told* you," Jessica said, "that only works on black people."

"How come you get to make those kinds of jokes?" Marc whined.

"Think about it, Marc," she replied patiently.

"Get out of my house, you rotten undead things!"

"She did the exact same thing when the Boy Scouts came around selling Christmas wreaths," I explained to the others, then took a step forward and snapped the cross away from her. "Where did you make this, shop class? You couldn't be bothered to go to a jewelry store and buy a nice one? I'm amazed you didn't make my dad cough up four figures for a diamond encrusted model."

"You get out of my house," she snapped. "You're not supposed to be able to do that."

"Tell me about it. Listen, we're going to ask you about my dad's other baby, and we're not leaving until you tell us everything."

"I'm not telling you rotten dead things a single detail. You're getting out and I'm going to sleep."

"Oh," Sinclair said, stepping forward once I'd put the popsicle sticks in my purse, "sleep will be the furthest thing from your mind in a few moments, Mrs. Taylor."

Chapter 7

I came back down to the living room after a refreshing five minutes of putting the Ant's perfumes in the dryer and pushing Spin. Antonia was sitting on the far end of the couch, leaning forward, and staring raptly into Sinclair's face. Her hands were palm down in her lap, and she was compulsively scratching at the leather, but she never looked away from his eyes.

I felt kind of weird about this whole thing. Why, exactly, were we doing this? I wasn't even sure how I felt about it, but here we were anyway, digging around the Ant's substandard brain. And why was Sinclair so interested? Didn't he have king stuff to worry about? A suit fitting somewhere? Jerk training to attend, or teach? But here he was, sitting on the denim footstool, holding the Ant's man hands in his and getting everything out of her. Everything.

". . . and then I tried to get him to propose, but he wouldn't do it, he was afraid Betsy would get mad at him if he left her mother, so we broke up."

"Yes, but the baby?" Sinclair asked.

"The baby . . . the baby . . ."

"Man, she is getting freaked," Marc muttered to me. "Look at her."

I looked. *Scratch, scratch* went her nails against her leather miniskirt, and the corner of her mouth was sagging like she'd had a stroke.

And I could smell her anxiety. It was like burning glue.

"I don't remember . . ."

"Antonia, you remember," Sinclair assured her. "You just haven't thought of it in many years. On purpose. Did the baby live?"

Her mouth hung open, and she moved her lips like she was trying to answer him, but nothing came out. Finally she groped and found Sinclair's hands, and the rest of her sordid tale just . . . just poured out. Like vomit.

"It wasn't me, it wasn't me! I got pregnant to get married, but it didn't work, and then the baby was here, and *it wasn't me!*" She wasn't just yelling, she was shrieking it, screaming it, and now her nails were digging into Sinclair's hands as she hung on for dear life. "It was supposed to work, and it *didn't work,* and I didn't know what happened, so I dropped her off . . . went to the hospital and left her in the lobby . . . nobody was around, but I knew someone would probably find her . . . so I put her down and never . . . never . . ."

"Jesus," I said, startled.

"The last time the Ant was this upset," Jessica whispered to me, "you came home a day early from summer camp."

"It's all right, Antonia," Sinclair soothed. "Of course it wasn't you. Who was it?"

"I don't know, I don't know." She bowed her head, and a dry sob escaped. "I was pregnant and then I wasn't and the baby . . . the baby . . ."

"Antonia, what day did you find out you were pregnant?"

"Halloween. Nineteen sixty-five."

"And what day was the next day? The day you woke up and the baby was already there?"

"August sixth, nineteen sixty-six. She was—she wasn't a newborn. I don't know how old she was, but she wasn't a newborn."

Dead silence while we all processed this. Marc hurried to Sinclair's side and whispered a question to him.

"Antonia, we're almost finished—"

"Good," she snapped, still looking at the floor. "I'm not telling you another thing."

"Yes, fine, Antonia, look up at me—that's better. Antonia, is there a history of mental illness in your family?"

"We don't talk about *that*."

"Of course not, only nasty people talk about *that*."

She was nodding so hard her hair actually moved. "Yes, that's right, that's exactly right, only nasty people—whiners, and—and—"

"But who was sick? In your family?"

"My grandmother. And both of my aunts. Not my mother, though, not *mine*."

"No, of course not. And you're different from them."

"It's just my nerves," she explained. "I just have very delicate nerves. *She* doesn't understand."

"No, she's not really the understanding type, is she?"

"Hey," I protested mildly.

"Anybody else would have stayed dead," the Ant went on, sounding aggrieved. "She didn't even have the class to do that. Has to be different—and—different—and has to rise and be a vampire. A vampire! She broke her father's heart."

"Class?" I yelped. "Oh, being undead is, what, classless now? And it's not like I had a choice, you tiny-brained, idiotic, shallow, Botoxed, gutless, chinless—"

"She lives with that rich Negro," the Ant confided. "And they're *not* married. Get what I'm saying?"

I slapped my forehead. Negro! Who even uses that word?

"I didn't know I was gay," Jessica commented.

Oh, Lord, let me die now again.

"Antonia, where did you leave the baby?"

"There was no baby."

"No, of course not. Certainly not *your* problem any-more. But where did you leave her?"

"She didn't cry when I left her," the Ant said steadily. "She was warm. I had—I had lots of towels and I could spare some. I put them in the dryer first."

"Of course you did, you're not a monster."

"*She's* the monster."

"Yes, she's terrible, and where is the baby?"

"Children's."

"Saint Paul," Marc whispered.

"All right, Antonia. You've been most helpful."

"Well, I try to donate to The Jimmy Fund when I go to the movies," she said.

"Oh, that's excellent. And you won't remember any-thing."

"No, I certainly will *not*."

"You'll go upstairs and get ready for bed. And you'll sleep like a baby."

"Yes, like a baby."

"Like the baby you callously abandoned," he said and abruptly let go of her hands.

* * *

"A sad woman," Sinclair commented when we were all outside again.

"Very sad," Tina agreed. She glanced at me out of the corner of her eye, which was as creepy as it sounded. "Very difficult."

"I've got privileges at Children's," Marc said. He was well into junior Sherlock Holmes mode, I was annoyed to see. "I bet we can track this baby down. And I bet I can get a crack at the Ant's med recs, too. Or at least try. I can try."

"Why do you want to see *her* records?" I asked. We weren't ready to get in the car yet, so we were sort of loitering outside on the front lawn.

"Because nobody blacks out for ten months unless something is *really* wrong. You heard her. One minute she was pregnant, the next she 'woke up' with a crying baby. So . . . what happened during that ten months?"

"I think I know," Tina said quietly.

"Tina," Sinclair said.

"Eric," she replied. She almost never used his first name.

"Tina?" I was surprised. Tina hadn't looked this nervous when Nostro threw us into the pit with the Fiends. But she was younger then. In a manner of speaking. "Hey, are you all right? Did you forget to have a snack?"

I noticed she had knotted her fingers together like kids playing "this is the church, this is the steeple" and now spoke to her knuckles, fast, without pausing. "My Queen,

I always liked you personally, but now I am filled with admiration because you're not psychotic after being raised by *that woman*."

"Awww," I replied. I almost smirked. "That gets me right here, Tina."

"It's true," Sinclair said. "It's a miracle you're not *more* vain, shallow, and ignorant."

"Thanks," I said. Then, "What?"

Chapter 8

"Wow!" Jessica said, shaking her head. "I heard it with my own ears, and I still don't believe she did it. Man, that's cold. Even for her."

"Most disagreeable," Sinclair agreed.

"Well . . ." Marc hesitated, then dunked his cookie into his tea until half of it dropped into the cup with a small plunk. Yech! I could never understand why he drank his cookies instead of eating them. "I'm not the biggest fan of Betsy's dad and stepmom, but if Antonia had a family history of that sort of thing—fugues or whatever—think how she must have felt. One minute she's pregnant, the next she's lost almost an entire year."

He shook his head. "She must have been scared shitless."

"Anybody would have been," I added, "but her especially because of her family history." I noticed everyone was staring at me. "What? I can put myself in her shoes. Her tacky, plastic shoes. I don't like her, and I definitely don't think she should have dumped my kid sister off in a hospital lobby, but I still feel kind of bad for her."

"Humph," Jessica said. She wasn't eating or drinking anything, just sitting at the table with the rest of us, her bony arms folded over her chest. "Listen, Tina, you were saying you thought you knew what happened the nine months the Ant was non compos mentis?"

Tina didn't say anything. After a moment, it got awkward.

"Uh, Tina? Hello?"

Sinclair sighed.

"Uh-oh," Marc said to his tea.

"Elizabeth," he began. "There is something I must tell you."

I carefully set down my cup. This never, *ever* boded well. It was never 'I bought you six dozen flowers and forgot you don't like yellow.' It was always stuff like 'By the way, now you're the queen' or 'Hey, I'm moving in.'

"Hit me," I said. I would have taken a deep breath to brace myself, but that would have just made me dizzy.

"This is . . . a private matter."

"Right," Marc said, standing and pulling Jessica out of her chair. "We'll just go."

"Right," Jessica said, catching on. "We'll, uh, be dusting something. In one of the rooms." They hurried out, and I heard her whisper, "She'll tell us later anyway."

"Possibly not," Tina said.

"I had an ulterior motive when we went to your stepmother's house."

"You *did*? *You* did? An ulterior motive? *You?* No way!"

"The Book of the Dead talks about your sibling."

"How do you know? I thought if you read that thing too long, you lost your mind."

"I have been reading bits and pieces of it over the last several decades."

I digested that one. "Okayyyyyy. So the Book knew I had a sister roaming around the wilds of wherever." Then it hit me, what he was saying. "*You* knew I had a sister."

"Yes."

"You knew I had a sister." I guess I felt like if I said it out loud enough, it would be less painful? "You *knew* I had a *sister.*"

"Yes. Until today, I had thought the sibling in question was the baby your stepmother is carrying now." Then he added, totally calmly, "I was working my way up to telling you."

"Eric!" Jessica shouted from the hallway. "Work *with* me!" She raced in, Marc on her heels. "What is the *matter* with you? I fix it so you can move in, but this is the sort of thing that makes her nuts. Crazy, *in*sane!"

"I think it's safe to say," I said through numb lips, "that I'm feeling a little insane right now."

"It's just that you had so many other things to worry about," Tina said quickly, trying to cover Sinclair's ass as usual. "Being sovereign and solving the murders from this summer and the—the house situation and the other vampires not respecting your position and all of that. That's why he had to go to Eur—never mind. He—we felt you had enough on your plate without worrying about your sister being the daughter of the devil and taking over the world."

I had been holding my teacup in both hands and accidentally squashed it like a bug. Jessica winced. Marc just stared at all of us. *"What?"*

Tina bit her lip. "Oh dear."

"Thank you for your assistance," Sinclair replied dryly.

Jessica dumped the cookies and crackers off the silver tray, walked around the table, and cracked Sinclair over the head with it. With a hollow *bonnnng!*, the silver dented. Sinclair didn't turn, just kept his steady, dark gaze on me.

"Lower," I said.

"You're so evicted," she told him.

Chapter 9

It was going to be sunrise soon enough, so I figured I should change into shorts and a T-shirt. What I really wanted to do was talk to Jessica about all that had happened that night, but she'd disappeared after assaulting Sinclair. There was still time to track her down . . .

I decided to cheer myself up by wearing my bargains, a $180 pair of white-and-black loafers. I'd be the best-dressed dead girl in the house. Then when I rose tomorrow night, I'd be ready for action. What kind of action, I had no idea. I'd worry about that then.

Meanwhile, I paired the bargains with black anklets, a black and white skirt, my cashmere mock turtleneck (a gift from Jess . . . the thing was practically indestructible in the hands of a good dry cleaner), and my black wool blazer. I checked myself out in the mirror and thought: adorable. I immediately felt better.

I guess this sounds kind of shallow, but it's harder to be depressed when you put yourself together as best you can. To put it another way, my life might be in the toilet again, but with my hair combed, my eye shadow coordinated, and my bra matching my underpants, I was ready for whatever the world threw at me.

I walked out of my room, down the stairs, down about six hallways, and into the kitchen, where Marc was eating Cheerios. I could hear Jess rummaging around on the other side of the room.

Without looking up from his cereal he said, "Nope."

I trudged back to my room, but not so quickly I couldn't hear Jessica talking to Marc.

"What was that? Where'd she go? I was looking for her."

"She's too tall to pull off the schoolgirl thing."

"I thought she looked cute."

"She looked like a blond zebra. Look, I'm her friend; it's my job to tell her this stuff."

"It's your job to pay rent. It's *my* job to tell her that stuff. You're a picky bitch," Jessica replied.

"Now who's spouting clichés? I'm gay so I'm bitchy?"

"No, you're gay *and* you're bitchy. I think she's had a tough enough week. And it's only Tuesday!"

"Right, so the last thing she needs is a fashion clashin' . . ." He trailed off (or I got far enough away) and I shut my bedroom door.

Nuts. Well, switch to leggings, stick with the mock and the blazer, and change into sandals. No, it was thirty degrees outside. Not that I was going outside. But you weren't really dressed until your toes had something under them. Penny loafers, I guessed.

I was just putting my bargains back into the closet when there was a knock at my door.

"Come in, Jess."

"Well, I thought you looked cute," she said by way of greeting.

"I think he's right. I'm too tall. You'd look good in that outfit. You want it?"

"No thanks. I want to talk about what happened earlier—" She glanced out the window. "You got time?"

"Yeah, half an hour, at least." I never saw the sun, though it couldn't hurt me. One of the perks of being the vampire queen. "Ugh, how awful was that whole thing?"

"No wonder Sinclair was so interested in tagging along tonight," she added, sitting next to me on the bed. "He knew, and he didn't tell you. Didn't warn you or anything."

"I *know*! See, see? Everyone's all 'Oh, give Sinclair a chance, he's not so bad' because they don't see the evil, dark, yukky, nutty side of him. He is the Almond Joy of my life."

"Honey, I'm convinced. That was pretty sneaky, even for him. Are you okay? It must have been a shock. You want another cup of tea or something?"

"No." I wanted not to be dead, but of course that wasn't happening anytime soon. No point bitching about it right that minute. But knowing me, I'd get back to it later. "I'm so full of tea I'm seeping. Thanks for smacking him for me."

"It was either bonk him on the head or stab him with his own butter knife."

"That could have been fun. And thanks for evicting him."

"I don't think it'll work." She frowned. "He won't leave."

"Vampires and cockroaches. They're impossible to get out of the ducts."

"So, what? What does this mean?"

"I have no idea. I was starting to get used to the Ant being knocked up."

"Lie."

"Okay, you're right, I was still kind of freaked. But now I'm sort of getting used to the idea that I've got another sibling, never mind that she's the daughter of the devil. Not the Ant. The *devil*. But—and stop me if you've heard this before—what am I supposed to do about it?"

Jessica shrugged.

"There's gotta be more to it than that. I suppose I'll have to go to him and get the rest of the story."

"Screw that."

"Amen." I flopped down onto my bedspread. "I knew it was too quiet around here," I mumbled into my pillow. "Something was bound to happen. I was expecting zombies to come out of the walls or something."

"Bets, I think it's time."

"No."

"Yes, it is. You need it, and you're ready."

"It's too soon."

"I know it's scary," she said, rubbing my back, "but you'll feel better. You know it's the right thing to do."

"I'm not ready," I replied, scared.

"Yes. You are. It's okay, I'll be there with you."

I shook my head, but she wouldn't be dissuaded.

The next evening . . .

"Oh my *Gawd*," the pedicurist said. "*What* have you been *doing* with your *feet?*"

"She's been dead for the last six months," Jessica said helpfully from the opposite chair.

"I don't *care*, that's no *excuse*. Gawd, they're like *hooves*. You've got to take better care of them. What about that cucumber cream I gave you last spring? It doesn't apply *itself*, y'know."

"I've been busy," I said defensively. "You know, with stuff." Solving murders. Trying to run Scratch. Restraining myself from jumping Sinclair's bones. Not that I wanted to do that anymore. I think it would be fair to say my desire for him had been thoroughly squashed. I didn't want those big hands on me or those firm lips on me or that big—anyway, squashed, thoroughly squashed.

"Everybody's got stuff, you've *got* to take care of your *feet."*

"And they'll take care of you," Jessica and I chorused obediently.

The pedicurist was sawing at my heels with a pumice stone. "Right! See, girls, you listen to me. Never mind about *stuff.* Foot care *has* to come first."

"Uh-huh." Maybe I could take her a little more seriously if she'd been out of high school more than twenty minutes. "I'll keep it in mind."

"Okeydokey then."

Jessica rolled her eyes at me, and I grinned back. "For a rich girl, you've got tough feet."

"Off my case, blondie. Yours aren't better."

"Yeah, but—"

"Didn't we just establish that there's nothing—not a single thing—more important than foot care?"

"Give me a break," I muttered.

The pedicurist dipped my feet back in the swirling

water, then shook the bottle of nail polish. "Good choice," she told me.

"I like the classics," I replied. Revlon's Cherries in the Snow. A great, dark red. I didn't like dark colors on my fingernails, but I liked them on my toes all right.

"There, now," Jessica sighed as her pedicurist rubbed her toes. "Told you. You needed this."

"I'm not arguing. Heck, for a couple of minutes I forgot about the whole my sister is a child of Satan thing."

"How are *her* feet?"

"Not as good as yours," I told the girl, which was probably the truth.

When I rose the next night, my feet were bare and unpolished. Unpumiced. They looked exactly the way they had the day I died.

I cried for five minutes—not over my stupid toes but for what it meant—and then I went downstairs and locked myself in the library with the Book of the Dead.

Chapter 10

I picked up the wing chair from beside the fireplace (carefully . . . the thing was probably ten times older than me) and jammed it under the doorknob. It wasn't likely anyone was going to come looking for me—Tina and Sinclair were avoiding me entirely, and Marc and Jessica were probably asleep—but I wasn't taking any chances.

I was pretty damned sick of, "Oh, did I forget to tell you? That was in the Book of the Dead, too." I was going to sit down with the awful fucking thing and read it cover to cover. No more surprises. No more worrying about Sinclair holding out on me.

No having to go to Sinclair to get the whole story.

I picked the thing up off the stand, already grossed out.

It was bound in human skin, how perfectly yuck-o, and felt warm to the touch, though that was probably because it was only a few feet away from the fireplace.

The Book. If the Bible was the Good Book, then this thing was the Terrible Bad Book. It supposedly had all sorts of vampire factoids within its nasty binding, and Sinclair had rescued it from his blazing mansion and stuck it in my house. We all avoided it like nobody's business. At least, I used to think so. But apparently Sinclair had been coming in the library and reading bits of it now and then. And keeping the good parts to himself, the treacherous prick.

I sat down, looking at the cover for a moment. *Tabla Morto*. The Book of the Extremely Creepy. Was that Latin? I didn't know from Latin. I peeked in the back . . . Was there an index? Could I look up "Betsy's sister" and save a lot of time? Nope, just a bunch of really disturbing pictographs back there. Never mind; I wasn't here to save time, I was here to save aggravation.

Chapter one, page one, here I come.

I wasn't scared. It was just a book. It couldn't hurt me. Nothing could hurt me. Except stupid Sinclair. No, that wasn't true. I was mad because he was keeping secrets, that was all. My king shouldn't keep secrets. *The* king shouldn't keep secrets, is what I meant.

The king. Sure. Some king. Fat lot of help he was to

me, or anybody. Okay, there was that whole fighting for my crown and almost dying incident, but he wanted power, not me. He knew stuff, private stuff about me, but instead of sitting down for a helpful chin-wag *with me,* he kept secrets and was all, "Don't read the Book too long in one sitting or you'll go insane." If that didn't work when I was a freshman in bio, it wasn't going to work now.

"Shalt be Vampyres and shalt be a Queen and King of Vampyres. But first the Vampyres will have no rule and shalt be chaos for twelve and a thousand yeares."

Right, right, I was following. That was Nostro and all the other little tin-pot dictators making Fiends and generally being disgusting. There really weren't any bosses until Sinclair and I came along. Which was weird, if you sat down and thought about it. Human beings had always had bosses . . . kings, queens, presidents, loan officers. Vampires managed to avoid them, by accident or design, until I came along.

See, what happened was, one vampire would intimidate and torture a bunch of others until he or she was ostensibly in charge, until another, jerkier one came along, and the whole thing started all over again.

Maybe they weren't so different from humans after all.

"After chaos shalt be the Pretender, destined to dust. A Queen shall ryse, who has powyer beyond that of the vampyre. The thyrst shall not consume her, and the cross never will harm her, and the beasts will befryend her, and she will rule the dead. The Pretender shalt overstep and the Queen will overcome."

Hmm, how 'bout that? I shallll overrrrrcommme . . .

"And the first who shall noe the Queen as a husband noes his Wyfe shall be the Queen's Consort and shall rule at her side for a thousand yeares.

"And the Queen shall noe the dead, all the dead, and neither shall they hide from her nor keep secrets from her."

Yeah, yeah, I knew all this. Tina and Sinclair had told me this around the time Nostro bit true dust. And what they didn't tell me I found out on my own—apparently I could see ghosts. Unlike Haley Joel Osment's claims, they *did* know they were dead.

As for keeping secrets, the Book of the Yukky was wrong, wrong, wrong. That's all the dead did these days.

"The Queen's sister shalt be Belov'd of the Morning Star, and shalt take the Worlde."

Beloved of the morning star? I figured that was fancy talk for the devil. Take the world? Take it where? Take it over? Ack! So not only did I have a secret evil sister, but she was fated to take over the world, just like I was fated to rule the vampires with Sinclair?

Damn. Quite the family tree. What was up with my dad's genetics?

And what was the big deal? Why not tell me? Okay, it sounded bad when you just blurted it out: "You're the queen; if you have sex with me, I'm the king; your sister is the devil's daughter and might or might not take over the world. Cream and sugar?" But was that really so fucking hard to say?

I was starting to get a headache, which wasn't uncommon since I had been reading for . . . what? I looked at my watch. Jesus, I'd been locked in here for three hours! And I'd read maybe ten pages. I didn't have this much trouble with an Umberto Eco novel.

It was the text. It was almost impossible to read this archaic crap which, I might add, had never been spell checked.

And the headache. How could I concentrate when my head was throbbing like a fucking rotten tooth?

But you don't get headaches anymore.

It was so fucking hard to concentrate.

You haven't had a headache since you became a vampire.

The light in here was bad, too. In fact, the light was fucking terrible.

A Vampyre.

Queen this and Vampyre that and secret sisters; it was all such a payn in the ass.

The Queen of the Vampyres.

Well, back to it. This nice warm book—at least my hands weren't cold for a change—wasn't going to memorize itself.

"... and the Morning Star shalt appear before her own chylde, shalt help with the taking of the World, and shalt appear before the Queen in all the raiments of the dark."

But it is nothing to worry about. In fact, you need not worry about a thing. Not one thing. The devil won't be as bad as you think; mostly that whole Lord of Lies thing is all hype.

And your sister might be a problem, but nothing you can't handle. What you should really handle is Eric Sinclair, because while he's a pain in the ass, he's also going to come in pretty handy, so you should stay on his good side.

Also, why are you wasting your time with all the sheep? For crying out loud. This is your damn house, and the sooner the lice crawling around on top of it figure it out, the better.

Hmm. For an evil book written by an insane vampire who could see the future . . .

How did I know that?

. . . written in blood and bound in human skin, this thing was making a lot of sense.

So just do your job . . . be the boss, run things your way, and rip the throat out of anyone who forgets who's in charge.

You know, I *had* been letting things slide a little.

I couldn't believe I'd been worried about reading the Book of Good Sense! Finally, I was seeing things clearly. It was all so obvious. The first thing I had to do was go down to Scratch and tell Slight Overbite that he'd been 100 percent right about the best way to run a vampire watering hole. Then I'd—

"Betsy! Are you in there? What are you doing?" *Wham Wham Wham!* "There's something wrong with the door!"

—clean up my house. That was so fucking typical. Nothing going on in this room was any of Jessica's damned business, but she was nosing around banging on doors and demanding answers. I'd been putting up with it for too long, and I was done now.

I got up from the small couch, slapped the book closed, laid it tenderly on the stand, and walked over to the door.

"Bets! What's going on? Are you okay? You're not doing anything weird and vampirey in there, are you?"

I grabbed the chair blocking the door and tossed it so hard it crashed into the far side of the room. I noticed I'd yanked it so roughly it had bent the knob. Oh well. Plenty more where those came from.

I jerked the door open.

"Is everything—" Her eyes widened. "Are you okay?"

"Fine," I said, then slapped her so hard her head banged against the doorframe and bounced off. She staggered and almost lost her feet, grabbed for my shoulder to steady herself, thought better of it, and leaned against the door. One hand flew to her cheek, and the other flew to the side of her head. I smelled the blood before I saw it start to trickle through her fingers.

"Betsy, wh—why—wh—"

"Don't bother me when I'm working again, or you'll get another one."

"But—b—b—"

"And I wouldn't advithe interrupting me, either," I told her sweetly. Her eyes were so big, her fear was so big. It was awesome. And ohhhhh, the blood. Just going to waste running through those annoying veins. I smacked her again, and it was kind of funny to see she couldn't dodge it in time, didn't even know my hand had moved until her other cheek started to throb. "I have to thay, I thould have done thith yearth ago."

"Betsy, what's *wrong*?" she cried, and I decided not to kill her. She was irritating, and I'd probably get her money when I pulled her head off—she didn't have any family—but even though she was scared shitless, she was wondering what was wrong with me.

What is *wrong with you?*

I decided I would keep her around; it'd be good to have a sheep who worried about my well-being no matter what I did to her.

And ohhhh, the blood. Did I mention the blood just going to waste?

"Nothing'th wrong," I told her, almost laughing at her terrified expression. "Not one thingle thing." Then I seized her shoulders, jerked her toward me, and took a big yummy chomp out of the side of her neck.

She screamed, and her hands came up, too late—way too late. It almost took the fun out of it; she was so slow. Her hands beat against me while I drank, but I didn't even feel it; instead I was thinking, *Blood taken by force tastes better.* It was weird, but there it was. I didn't make the rules.

I let her go when I was done, and she hit the carpet so hard she raised a cloud of dust. She crawled away from me, sobbing, and curled up under one of the end tables. I licked her blood from my fangs and felt them retract . . . one of these days I was going to get the hang of this, by God. Sinclair could make his come and go whenever he wanted.

Ummm . . . Sinclair.

"So, let's recap," I told her, bending down so I could see her under the table. "Don't interrupt me when I'm working, don't cut me off . . . really, just leave me alone unless I need you. In fact, it's probably better not to speak until spoken to. I'm glad we had this little chat," I finished cheerfully. It was good to get the new ground rules out into the open. "I'll see you later. Oh, and I'll need a check for three thousand dollars. There's a sale at Marshall Field's."

I left, carefully shutting the library door behind me. Oh, goody, the doorknob worked, even if it was bent on the inside. I should reward myself for not wrecking it.

Make it four thousand dollars.

Chapter 11

I bumped into Marc on the way to my room to get shoes and car keys. He was scruffy (it was amazing how someone with such brutally short hair constantly looked like he needed a comb) and his scrubs were a mess.

"Why are you here?" I asked him.

"I'm pulling a double tomorrow, so Dr. Abrams let me knock off early." He peered at me. "You've got blood on your—"

"No," I said, "I mean, why are you *here?* Sucking off me like a big leech? You've only got your father, he's *sick,* but instead of tending to *your* business you're hanging around here butting into *my* business, paying—what?—two hundred bucks a month to live in a mansion? You hate your

95

job, you hate your life, you haven't had a *date* in all the time I've known you, never mind a relationship, and the only way you can feel like you're worth anything is to tag along on vampire errands. Pathetic, Dr. Spangler. Really really lame."

He was gaping at me, which was pretty funny. Finally he said, "I don't hate my job."

Good comeback . . . not! "Move, Dr. Leech," I said, and shoved past him. Lucky for him I was full. I made a mental note to throw his ass out tomorrow, after he'd had a day to mull over each and every truthful observation I'd made. Maybe he and Jessica would get together and cry on each other's shoulders. That could be funny.

I got to my room and kicked my Manolos out of the way. Ridiculous! Teetery high heels—when would I wear lavender pumps? I'd thought to wear them when I married Andrea and Daniel, but not only were they totally stupid shoes to wear in my position, I sure as shit wasn't going to let a vampire marry her sheep. They were food, not partners. What had I been thinking when I congratulated them? *Congratulated?*

I decided to take it easy on myself. Okay, I hadn't been thinking, in fact, I'd been running from my destiny. I hadn't figured it out then, but I had a handle on it now. It was the difference between being a young vampire and a queen.

I opened my closet door and pawed through the orderly piles of shoes. Yellow leather sandals—idiotic. Red knee-high boots—gaudy. Roger Vivier evening pumps beaded with turquoises. Turquoise! I hated turquoise, but I'd dropped almost a thousand bucks on a shoe decorated with that ridiculous rock. Fontenau heels in piss yellow . . . which I could only wear with black. Manolo Blahnik pumps in basic black . . . I could have gotten black pumps at Wal-Mart for twenty bucks!

Marabou mules. Emma Hope slippers. Japanese smiley face slippers—*smiley faces!* Leather golf cleats in tan and white . . . I didn't play golf. Cowboy boots . . . I didn't have a horse! I didn't even like to go out to the garden.

What was wrong with me? I'd pissed away thousands of dollars on stuff that went on my *feet*. My money problems would have been solved ages ago if I'd just stuck with flip-flops.

I finally found a pair of old green rubber boots I wouldn't be annoyed to be seen in and tugged them on, then clomped out the door in search of my purse. The mansion was worthy of my station, but it always took a while to get organized and out the door. Maybe I'd have elevators installed. And those concave mirrors they had in convenience stores. It would be nice to see who was coming down the hall.

Speaking of surprises, I rounded yet another corner and there was His Majesty King Sinclair coming toward me.

He was impeccably dressed in trademark temperate colors: dark slacks, black belt, black shirt, black wool greatcoat. The dark clothes made even his eyes seem black, like a starless night in the middle of winter; I couldn't tell where the irises stopped and the pupils began.

There was some color in his cheeks—not a chill from being outside like you'd expect from a regular guy, but because he'd recently fed. I wondered who he'd bitten. Normally I tried not to think about it, but since he'd ditched the harem (in a needy attempt to get on my good side) he had to be hard up for blood.

Maybe he pounced on muggers and rapists, like I did. Of course, due to recent eye-opening events, I was a little more broad-minded now about the quality of victims. Really, if they were on the street, they were fair game. It's not like they died from it or anything. Well, they might now. But I had other things to worry about.

"You're looking yummy," I said, reaching out as he neared and stroking the lapel of his coat. "As usual."

"So are . . . you . . ." he replied slowly, stopping in mid-stride and giving me a closer look. "You smell like blood. You've spilled some on your shirt."

"Silly me."

"And are those rubber boots?"

I edged closer. "Don't you think there are more interesting things for us to talk about than footgear?"

His gorgeous brow wrinkled. "Er . . . well, yes, frankly, but—"

I pulled him close and kissed him on the mouth. His firm, yummy mouth. Ooofa. How had I kept my hands off him all these months? His room was five doors down from mine, not five miles.

His hands were instantly all over me, slipping up the back of my turtleneck and clutching my shoulders. Oh, good, he wasn't going to be difficult.

I ripped through his coat and shirt, and we lurched back and forth in the hallway, clothes tearing, tongues exploring. We crashed through a door—and I don't mean we bumped into it and it flew open. I mean we left splinters and fell over a chair or something— I dunno, I wasn't taking a fucking inventory, I didn't even know what room we were in—and then we were rolling around on the dusty carpet.

His throat was right over my mouth while his hands were busy below my waist, tearing through my clothes to give himself access, and I couldn't resist and bit him. He stiffened above me, and I nearly groaned as his warm sweet/salty blood filled my mouth. His hands moved faster, the tearing got louder, and then he was shoving his way inside me, filling me up, and I rose to meet him and then pulled back from his neck.

I licked his throat, and he seized me by the hair, jerked my head to one side, and sank his fangs into my neck. His rough urgency shoved me over into orgasm, and I brought my knees up and met him thrust for thrust. I had another one and was trying for big number three when he shuddered and his head dropped to my shoulder.

"So," I said after a moment, "you're gonna need a new coat."

He laughed. "Among other things."

I stuck out my arm and looked at my watch over his shoulder. "Well, we've got about an hour until the sun comes up. I was gonna run down to Scratch, but I guess I could do that tomorrow."

"Is it time for the tiresome small talk?"

"I was thinking it was time for the oral sex."

He rolled off me, jumped to his feet, picked me up in his arms, and galloped to my room.

Chapter 12

"Dare I ask what prompted this change of heart?" he asked after slamming the door shut with his heel and dumping me in the middle of the bed.

"It's boring," I replied, removing the shreds of my clothes. "Besides, you shouldn't look a gift horse in the crotch."

"A cliché that should be cross-stitched onto a sampler, no doubt." He was hopping on one foot as he frantically tried to remove his shoe, and I laughed at the sight.

I had a thought, there in my head and almost gone, but I groped for it and got it. I wondered why I hadn't been able to read Sinclair's mind during sex, as I had always been able to do so before.

Well, my head had been a lot emptier before. There was room for him in there while we were boning away. But there wasn't room for him anymore. That was all right with me, though. A lot of things were going to be different from now on.

Finally he was rid of the stupid things and joined me on the bed. "I am glad you're here," he told me. "I've waited a long time."

"Lover, the waiting's over. I think it's safe to say I'm finally in a position to appreciate all your excellent qualities."

And speaking of positions, we sixty-nined for a while—the cool thing about being a vampire? You don't need to stop to catch your breath. He was all the way down my throat and it didn't bother me a bit. We'd have to find someone to come in and fix the headboard, though . . . it was cracked right down the middle. One of us had kicked it—well, at one point we'd both kicked it.

After a while I climbed on top of him (Heigh-ho Silver, awaaaaay!) and was happily bouncing my way toward yet another orgasm when I heard the unmistakable sound of a car pulling into the drive.

"Who's that?" I asked, looking at my watch again. Hmm. Fifteen minutes until sunrise. Vampire?

"Tina," he groaned. "Do you think you could focus on the matter at hand, darling?"

Tina! Little Miss "You're the Queen but Sinclair's my boy" backstabber. So quick with the "Your Majesty" routine and so quick to sabotage me, leave me in the dark, do anything she could, every damn time, to make sure Sinclair came out on top.

I needed *him;* I sure as shit didn't need her. She was old—the oldest vampire I knew—and she was dangerous.

I had to get rid of her.

I dismounted and groped for my robe, which was hanging off the door to the master bath. No time to get properly dressed; I wanted to take care of this *now.*

"Elizabeth!" Sinclair sounded equal parts aggrieved and surprised. "Do you have an appointment you've forgotten?"

"Yeah." *Just a little something I should have done six months ago.* "I'll be back. Don't finish without me."

"But—" I was already hurrying down the hallway and didn't hear the rest. Sex with him was always super, and I'd get back to it soon enough, but this was a lot more important. The last thing I needed in my house was an infinitely old, infinitely crafty vampire who didn't have my best interests at heart.

Besides, there were plenty more where she came from. Younger. Less dangerous. Certainly less annoying. And my boy Sinclair wasn't going anywhere. He practically had a leash and a collar.

I caught up with Tina in the front entryway; she had just shut the door. I guess I'd really jammed down those stairs.

"Good morning, Your M—" Then she screamed. Possibly because I'd taken the small gold cross out of my robe pocket and thrown it at her.

Sinclair had given me the delicate necklace a few months ago (it had formerly belonged to his ages-dead baby sis). I couldn't wear it around the house; it hurt Sinclair and Tina to look at it, not to mention any vampire who wanted to come calling.

But (and this is the dopey part) I liked to keep it close. So it was usually in the pocket of my jeans or, at bedtime, my robe.

"Tina, in case you haven't noticed, I've had just about enough of your shit."

"Don't—don't—" She'd dodged and was cringing in the corner. "Don't do that!"

"Don't ever tell me *don't*." Hmm, that had sounded more menacing in my head. Oh well. She'd catch up with current events soon enough. Out with the old, in with the new. And all that.

"What's happened?" she cried.

I sent a fist looping toward her face for an answer, but she was too quick, and next thing I knew I was wrist-deep in the wall.

"Dammit!" I pulled my hand out and shook the plaster dust off. When I had someone call the headboard repairer, I'd also have them get a wallpaper hanger in here and have someone build a new door.

But first, back to the business at hand. I looked around for the cross. I could jam that sucker right through her forehead and bye-bye Tina; she'd die screaming and that was fine, as long as she died.

Ah! There it was, on the floor beside the small table we dumped our house keys on. I bent for it—and Tina grabbed my shoulder and pulled me back so hard I went sailing into the opposite wall.

"Hey!" Now I *really* wanted to kill her. "You keep your hands to yourself, you fucking cow."

"I'm sorry, Majesty." She was standing perfectly still, well to the left of the cross. She watched me carefully and with interest, like a cat watches a mouse hole. "But I'm not going to let you kill me. I want to help you. What's wrong?"

"Help me by standing still," I replied, and launched myself at her. And got a kick to the chest for my trouble, and broke a chair as I hit the ground.

Damn! "You've kept in shape the last hundred years or so."

"It's one of the advantages of being immortal," she said

calmly. It was actually sort of impressive how quickly she'd gone from flabbergasted surprise to cool assessment. Like I needed another reason to kill her. "Plenty of time to learn how to fight. What's happened?"

"Nothing much. Got some light reading done earlier tonight. The good news is, I know all about my sister. The bad news is, you're gonna have to go, Tina. Sorry."

"She's gone crazy, Tina, watch out." I looked. Jessica was standing in one of the doorways, gray-faced and bloody. She had a palm pressed to her forehead, stanching the yummy flow of blood. How had I let her sneak up on us? Son of a bitch! This house had too many people in it, and all but one or two were gonna have to go.

Jessica swayed a little and clutched the doorframe to steady herself. "I mean really crazy. I think—I think she read the Book for too long."

"I gathered. Oh, Majesty." Tina shook her head. "What are we going to do with you?"

This was annoying, to put it mildly. "You, shut the fuck up. And get lost; this is vampire business. And *you,* stand still." I crossed the room too quickly for Tina to see—except she did see and easily avoided me. That was okay; it brought me much closer to the cross. I bent to get it. I'd ax Tina, and then I'd tool up on Jessica so bad, she'd be more worried about her iron lung than ratting me out ever again.

I heard the *whoosh* a split second before I felt the impact. The sun must have come up early, because my skull was filled with light.

Then the sun fell down. And so did I.

Chapter 13

I groaned and opened my eyes. The hangover was incredible. Had I read a book or downed a liter of vodka?

The light made me blink, and I tried to process the eighty zillion thoughts rocketing through my head. There was one tiny bit of good to come out of the whole mess: I knew a lot more about the devil's daughter. But there were other issues I had to—

Wait a minute.

The *light*?

I looked. I was in a small room on the west side of the house; there was no furniture, but it had a good solid oak door. In fact, it was going to be the wine cellar until Sinclair pointed out that we couldn't keep wine in a room with so much light, the big know-it-all. So the bottles had been moved to the basement, and this room had stood empty and . . .

The light.

It was the sun.

I climbed to my feet—I was still in my robe—and walked over to the window.

The sun.

I stared. Then I stared some more. The big golden ball was just about level with the tree line; it looked like late afternoon to me.

I hadn't seen the sun since my thirtieth birthday, way back in April.

I'd read the Book of the Dead and let it turn me into a real asshole. That was bad. Very, very bad. But in return, I could now wake up when it was still daylight out. That was good. Very, very good.

And since I was the Queen and the sun didn't burn me, I could *go out*. Walk around and feel the light on my face, the warmth.

I tried to pull the window up, but it wouldn't budge. The mansion had so many rooms and there were so few people living in it, the window probably hadn't been opened in fifty years or more.

Too impatient to mess with prying, too wild to get outside, I broke the window with my fist and punched out the bigger pieces. Then I dove through it, feeling like Starsky. Or Hutch—which one was the blond again?

I thudded to the ground two stories below, spat out the dirt, and flopped over on my back to soak up the sunshine. The grass was chilly (it was a mild October for Minnesota, but it was still October), but I didn't care. The sun wouldn't be up much longer, but I didn't care. I had some tall apologizing to do, but—well, I cared about that, and I'd get right to it, too.

In a minute.

Thank you, God. Thank you so much! I totally don't deserve it. But thanks all the same.

Thoughts of the previous evening's activities kept crowding into my brain, wrecking my sunbathing. Unfortunately for me, the Book didn't provide amnesia.

Last night's itinerary flashed through my mind. Trying to kill Tina—who had handily kicked my ass. It was embarrassing to get stomped by someone half my size, but I was glad I hadn't succeeded. Those awful things I'd said to Marc . . . He'd been a good friend to me, and I'd called him Dr. Leech.

And Jessica . . . *Oh, Jess. I screwed up so bad. I'd set myself on fire before I'd hurt you again. You're the best friend a vampire could have.* Yeah, that sounded good. Repeat as needed. And repeat. *God, if she just hears me out, I'll apologize for the next thirty years. Just please, please let her listen.*

And Sinclair. I groaned and threw an arm over my eyes. Skanky villain sex with Eric Sinclair! That was almost as bad as feeding off of Jessica. I was mad at myself for using him and mad at him for letting me do it.

And for *not noticing* I was evil! How could that little fact escape his attention? The sucker noticed when a fly landed a block away, but he didn't realize I'd turned into SuperBitch?

I sat up, annoyed and dismayed, and heard the unmistakeable *cha-chik!* of a shotgun shell being chambered. I'd been on enough duck hunting trips with my mom to know what that sounded like. (Those were my pre-PETA days, just like now was post-PETA; they were getting a little extreme for my taste.)

I looked around. Marc was standing about twenty yards away, holding my old twelve-gauge. What was that statistic? More people who kept guns in their home were fated to be the victims of that gun than victims of other violence?

Since I was right in his sights, I silently vowed to pay more attention to such statistics in the future.

"Uh, I'm not dangerous anymore," I said.

"Mmmm," he replied. He wasn't wearing scrubs or shoes, just jeans and a Tori Amos T-shirt. He either didn't have work or he'd taken the day off to deal with his psychotic undead roommate. "You all right? Did you cut yourself going out the window?"

He wanted to know if I was all right! It was almost enough to make me overlook the shotgun. "No. I mean, no, I didn't cut myself, not no, I'm not all right. I *am* all right. Now, I mean."

"Eric heard you go out."

"Okay. Uh, what are you planning on doing with that thing?"

"Well." He took a step closer, but the barrel didn't waver. "It won't kill you, but we figured it would slow you down. You can dodge bullets, but Tina doesn't think you can dodge buckshot."

"Tina's probably right. Is she okay?"

"Sure." He smirked a little. "She won the fight, in case you don't remember."

"I remember." I sighed and rested my head on my knees. "I remember everything, unfortunately. I guess now's a good time to start with the groveling. I'm sorry for what I said to you, Marc." I looked up at him. "I didn't mean it. I'd be pretty upset if you moved out."

"Uh-huh."

"Really, Marc. I'm really sorry. I screwed up."

"Okay." The gun stayed up.

"Is—is everybody else inside?"

"Yeah. Tina's still resting, but Eric and Jess and I are all awake. We were trying to figure out—never mind."

Trying to figure out what to do with me when the sun

went down and I was still evil. I almost smiled; bet Sinclair didn't expect me to get up at four o'clock in the afternoon.

"It wasn't much of a prison cell," I couldn't help pointing out. "It had a glass window."

"We were counting on the effects wearing off."

"Well, is it okay if I go in?"

At last, the shotgun came down a little. "What are you going to do?"

"Grovel until I make it right. Oh, and yell at Sinclair. You believe he didn't notice I was psycho?"

"Yeah, well . . . he's kind of upset, too."

"*He's* upset?"

"Yeah."

I couldn't help but notice Marc hadn't put the safety on. He might believe I was back to myself, but he wasn't going to take any chances. It made me sad; he'd never been especially wary around me before.

I wondered what else had changed.

Chapter 14

"Look who's feeling better!" Marc called as I hesitantly entered one of the tea rooms.

"Uh, hi," I said. Then, "What is *that* doing in here?"

I didn't mean Sinclair (though, after last night, I wasn't especially thrilled to see him, either). I was pointing to the Book of the Dead which, incomprehensibly, was on the table next to the bowl of sugar cubes.

"I, too, decided to do some light reading," Sinclair replied. He looked like he was playing statues; he was sitting stiff as a board. "Of course, I stopped after a couple of pages."

"Look, you were right, okay? I shouldn't have read it. Big, dumb, lame mistake."

"Really dumb," Marc added helpfully.

"Really dumb," I agreed, still looking at Sinclair. "And you shouldn't have had sex with me."

"*You* had sex with *me*," he pointed out, having the nerve to sound annoyed. "And you left early."

"Well, yeah, because I was totally evil! And you didn't even notice!" Hmm, my groveling wasn't going quite the way I planned. Still, I couldn't help being upset. "How could you not notice?"

He stood. It was easy to forget what a big guy he was when he was sitting down all prim and proper at tea. But when he flashed to his feet—too quick for most people to track—he towered over everyone else. Marc actually flinched, not that I could blame him. I felt a little like flinching myself.

"I take it to mean," he said quietly, "that the only reason you chose intimacy with me—repeatedly—is because you were out of your head?"

"Well . . ." Boy, did that sound bad. And he looked—not crushed, but like he was getting ready to be crushed. "Uh . . . it's not like I don't think you're a great-looking guy, Eric. I don't think finding each other attractive has ever been the problem." I'd been so focused on what I'd done to Marc and Tina and Jess, I hadn't really thought about how Eric might feel about it. I mean . . . he was a guy. He got laid. A couple of times! I thought he'd be generally okay with it and would scold me about the Book but . . . I didn't think I'd hurt his feelings. Hell, I didn't think I could hurt him at all.

He was the king of the vampires, for goodness' sake.

"Anyway . . ." I was still trying to figure out how to finish the sentence without hanging myself or hurting Eric worse than I already had.

"Oh, hey, look at this," Marc said too heartily. "A shotgun! This isn't mine. I'll just put it back in your closet, Betsy. Well, maybe *my* closet." Then he hurried out.

"Put the safety on when you unload it," I called after him.

"Never mind," Eric said quietly, and I whipped back around. He had sat down again when I wasn't looking. The moment, whatever it was, had passed. "You have answered my question, whether you meant to or not."

"Eric . . ."

"Elizabeth, it has not escaped my notice that you are awake."

"Right. Can't get anything past you." I sat down across from him. "I was outside getting some sun when Marc came to get me. I've got some tall apologizing to do, I know. Where's Tina?"

"Still resting." He was giving me the weirdest look.

"Until the sun sets, of course. You say you were *outside*? I heard the glass break but I could hardly believe—"

"Yeah. It was great! I wish you could come out with me; the sun felt so good."

"The sun would incinerate me in a nanosecond."

"Right. Sorry about that. I haven't been out during the day in six whole months, so I was glad to get out of here, believe me."

"Tina," he said, still looking at me like I was a strange new species of bug, "has not seen the sun in well over a hundred years."

"Well, I'll tell her all about it. After I, you know, make things right. Although I'm not sure how much I've got to make right with her; she *did* kick my ass pretty good. You should have seen it," I joked, trying to lighten the mood a little.

"I missed it, as I was waiting for you to return to bed," he said coldly, and I almost cringed.

"You—" I tried to fix it. Couldn't think of a way. I finished the sentence, hating how I sounded like a sad little kid instead of a grown woman. "You really didn't notice?"

"I was . . . distracted. I can assure you, it will never happen again."

His face was so still, so cold. I had to get out of there. Now. This very second. "Where's Jessica?"

"Hiding from you, of course." He grabbed the Book and

stood. "I should put this back. Since you appear to be back to yourself, there is no need for further research. Good day."

And that was that.

Chapter 15

"Jessica?" I softly tapped on the door with my knuckles. "Jess? It's Bets. Can I come in?"

Silence. I could hear her moving around in there, but she wasn't talking. Ugh. I could take anything—death, torture, knockoffs—but the silent treatment.

"Jess? I fucked up, honey. Really really bad. I'm so sorry. Sorry for hitting you and biting you and saying all those rotten things." Listing my sins made me feel worse, if possible. "Can I please come in?"

Nothing. And who could blame her? I wouldn't talk to me, either.

"Jess, let me in, sweetie. Wouldn't you rather see me

groveling in person? And I've got a good grovel going, you really don't want to miss it."

Nothing.

"Well." I coughed. "I wanted to tell you I'm not evil anymore and say I'm sorry for—you know. For everything. I'll—uh—I'll be around if you need to talk. Or something. Okay? Okay. Well, I'm gonna go now."

I paused, waiting for her to dramatically fling open the door and holler for me to wait. That's what always happened in the movies. Then I turned around and walked down the hall.

This was gonna be much, *much* harder than I thought. I'd fucked it up all the way around, all because I'd decided to read the Book of the Dead instead of rereading *Gone With the Wind*. I felt like Scarlett after the Yankees went through Tara, except less attractive.

Marc and Tina were at the foot of the stairs, talking. I resisted the urge to eavesdrop—I'd made enough mistakes in the last forty-eight hours—and slowly walked down to meet them.

"Feeling better, Majesty?" Tina asked. Her smile looked real. Marc seemed okay, too. His shoulders were a little set, but he looked relaxed enough.

"Um, yeah. Listen—"

"I'm glad you're all right now. And I must apologize for taking liberties with your person. I—"

I grabbed her little paws and looked down into her big pansy eyes. "Oh, Tina, I'm the one who owes *you* the apology. I suck!"

The corner of her mouth twitched as she attempted to extricate her hands. "Majesty, you do not."

"No, I totally do. I feel so bad that I tried to kill you. I'm *glad* you kicked my ass. Humiliated, but glad. I didn't know you could fight like that!"

She laughed and brushed her straw-colored bangs out of her eyes. "Luckily for me. I must admit, I had a bad moment when you threw your necklace at me."

"Well, I'm really sorry."

"I, also. I am glad," she added with touching sincerity, "you are better."

"Oh, I'm completely evil-free."

"And . . . you rose while the sun was up."

"Yeah. Turn evil, get a new power," I joked. "It's like the worst trade-off ever."

"Hmm," she replied, giving me the same look Sinclair had. It wasn't much fun when *she* looked at me that way, either.

"You should have seen her rolling around in the grass like a big blond puppy," Marc said. "It was pretty hilarious."

"You hush," I said, but I couldn't help smiling. It felt good after recent events.

Chapter 16

"**W**ell, I do have some good news!" I shouted. "I know how we can track down my sister!"

"Why are we having a meeting in the hallway?" Sinclair asked, looking up from his notes for practically the first time all night.

"So Jessica stays in the loop, duh," I replied. "Anyway, I thought we could track my long-lost sister down and ask her not to take over the world! Okay? I mean, something good came out of the fuckup du jour, right?!?"

Marc rubbed his ear. "How do you want to start?"

"Well, I know she was born right here in the Cities, on June 6, 1986!"

"Six six eighty-six?" Tina asked. "That's interesting."

"It's lame, is what it is! What, we're in *The Omen* now?!? But anyway, we can narrow it down to all the baby girls born to the Ant on six six eighty-six, and how many of them can there be? One, I'm guessing!"

"I don't think you have to *scream*," Marc said. "Her door isn't that thick."

"Do you think you can get the records? You said at the Ant's that you'd try!" This meeting was making me tired. And why wouldn't Sinclair look at me? I figured he was still pissed about the other night. Not a word about how he didn't even notice I was evil, natch. I started to get freshly annoyed and tried to squash it. I was in no position to play the victim. "Marc?!?"

"Shit, I heard you." He rubbed his ear. "Yeah, I don't think that'll be too hard."

"What about confidentiality issues?" Tina asked.

"What's that you say?" I shrieked. "You want to know how we get around confidentiality stuff?"

They both looked annoyed, and then Marc answered her. "Well, let's put it this way. Normally I don't like to go snooping around in charts that are none of my business. But to find Satan's daughter and save the world, I'll make an exception. And Tina, if you or Eric come with me, I'm sure we can get past the clerks."

"All right," Tina said.

"Do you want me to come, too?" I screamed.

"It's not necessary," Tina said, leaning away. "We'll tend to this errand for you, Majesty. Besides . . ." She eyed the closed, locked door to Jessica's bedroom. "You have other things to worry about."

"Right! Well, here's what happened! In case you were wondering!"

"*I'm* wondering how long this meeting will last," Sinclair muttered.

"The devil got really bored down there in Hell and decided to come to Earth for a while! And she possessed the Ant when she was knocked up! And then she went back to Hell!"

"You know all this?" he asked, looking up again.

"Yes! The Book told me! I mean, it didn't *tell* me, I sort of read about it and then just knew the rest!"

"So your stepmother actually *was* the devil for, what, almost a year?"

"Yes!"

"That's amazing," Tina said, wide-eyed.

"Not so amazing! What's amazing is that she was possessed by Satan for almost a year and nobody noticed anything unusual!"

What was that? I thought I'd heard a muffled laugh from the other side of the door. I listened hard, but I couldn't hear anything else. Nuts.

"I have to admit, that's a new one on me," Marc said. "But you don't seem surprised."

"I grew up with the woman. So the devil thought she was the perfect vessel . . . I guess you called it, Marc." My voice was getting tired, so I was talking normally for the moment. "She lost nearly a year of her life, and when she came back to herself, she must have totally freaked. Dumped the baby, tried to get things back to normal. Then later, she managed to talk my dad into marriage. So she got what she wanted, eventually."

"But at what cost?" Sinclair asked. He was sitting cross-legged on my right side and turned to give me a look that was almost scorching. Then the moment passed, and he was back to his notes.

"Right," I said uneasily. "Okay! So, Satan went back to Hell, the Ant broke up my parents' marriage, my sister was dumped into the foster care system, and now we gotta find her before she takes over the world!"

"An interesting agenda," Tina said, bringing up a small hand to cover her smile.

"For all the good it will do," Sinclair said, "your sister is fated to rule the world. As you will recall from your own late reading, there is not a lot of gray area in the Book. I doubt anything we can do will prevent the daughter of the devil from doing that which she pleases."

"Well, we're gonna try!" I hollered back. "We can't not try!"

He shrugged. "As you wish."

Damn right, as I wish. Now if I could just tear him away from his precious note-taking, things might start getting back to normal around here. What the hell was so damned engrossing, anyway? His last will and testament? His grocery list? I leaned over and peeked, but he was writing in a language I didn't know.

"Okay, meeting adjourned!" I shrieked. "Unless anybody has anything to add?" I half-turned and watched Jessica's door, but it didn't open.

So that was that.

The next afternoon, I drove to my mom's office at the U. Tina wasn't up yet, Jessica was still avoiding me, Marc was off somewhere, and if I was exposed to much more of Sinclair's cold shoulder, I was gonna get frostbite.

We'd find out later tonight what, if anything, Tina and Marc had found out, but for now, the waiting was driving me nuts. The whole situation was driving me nuts.

So, like any insecure, lonely, friendless vampire, I wanted my mommy.

She'd had the same dumpy office for twenty years—tenure

didn't mean a decorating budget, apparently—and I made my way there in no time. DR. ELISE TAYLOR, HISTORY DEPARTMENT was etched on the glass part of the door. Her specialty was the Civil War, specifically the battle of Antietam. Like I hadn't had my fill of *that* by the time I was ten.

I could hear her talking in the hallway long before I saw her silhouette against the door. She had half-opened it and was still haranguing her colleague:

"I'm not going to the thing, and you can't make me, Bob, you absolutely can't."

Then she saw I was waiting for her. Her mouth popped open, and her green eyes bulged. Her snow-white hair was straggling out of its usual neat bun; it was her post–sophomore Civil War 124 look. Then she shut the door on poor Bob and ran to me.

"Betsy! You're up!" She looked out her window, looked back at me, looked out the window again. "My God, what are you doing up?"

"Surprise," I said, holding out my arms. She jumped into them—I'd been a head taller since I was twelve—and gave me a squeeze. "I thought I'd do the pop-in."

"I love the pop-in if it's you. So what's happened? Is this part of being the queen? Oh!" Her hand went to her mouth. "I just realized . . . this means you can go to Antonia's baby shower."

I grinned. "Thanks. I totally hadn't thought of that until now. Heh."

"So . . . what's happened?"

I ended up telling her most of it: reading the Book, and going crazy, and what I had done to Jessica and Marc and Tina. I left out what I'd done to Sinclair. Mom didn't need any updates on my sorry sex life. Besides, she was so fond of Sinclair she'd probably be annoyed with me. I also left out the daughter of the devil angle. Mom was broadminded, but it was best to give her the info in digestible chunks.

". . . and Jess is still hiding from me—she sleeps at night now, behind a locked door. She used to stay up all night because I was up all night. I really screwed the pooch, Mom. Pardon my French. I think the worst part is, I'm in a mess that's totally of my own making. Sinclair warned me about the Book, but I didn't listen. And Jess paid for it. Everybody paid for it."

"You did, too, honey," my mom said, her eyes soft with sympathy. Ahhhh. A mother's love . . . it was like slipping into a sauna—warm, yet hard to breathe. "You're still paying for it. Of course, Jessica is upset. But you've been friends since the seventh grade. A little felony assault isn't going to change that."

"Do you think so?"

"Yes," she said firmly, and I started to perk right up. "Your friendship survived death. It'll recover from this. Just keep apologizing. Do it every single day. Besides, a little remorse will do you good, dear."

"Thanks, Mom."

"I take it Tina and Marc have forgiven you?"

"Yeah, seems like it. Tina never seemed mad about it in the first place, and Marc's a little tense around me, but he treats me nice and all. It's just Jessica." And Sinclair. But there was only so much I could stand to tell her about my own piss-poor behavior.

"Honey, it wasn't your fault. It was that Book. Bound in skin and written in human blood, you say? It must be ancient . . . possibly predating—well—everything." Her eyes were seeing me and far away at the same time; I'd seen that look before. "What I wouldn't give to—you say you keep it in your library?"

"Mom. Seriously. If I see you near that thing, I'll throw it in the fireplace. I might do it anyway. No Book for you." So she'd know I wasn't kidding, I went Soup Nazi on her. We were both gigantic *Seinfeld* fans. "*No Book for you!*"

"Betsy, you can't." She was all somber and reproachful. Not a big fan of book-burning, my mom. "It's literally priceless. Think of what we could—"

"It's a priceless pain in my big white butt. You don't go anywhere near it, get me? The thing's been around forever, and even Sinclair hasn't read it all—just enough to torture me with. I mean it, Mom. Promise you won't try to check it out."

"I promise if you promise not to burn it."

"Fine, I promise. And thanks for the escape hatch, but I can't blame the Book for how I acted after. Nobody stuck a gun in my ear and made me read it. It was my choice. And I've *got* to make it up with Jess."

"Well, keep trying to apologize. You'll have more time to do that, now." She looked out the window again.

I leaned down and rested my head on her shoulder. "Yeah, you're right. I'll keep at it."

She rubbed my back, and we watched the sun go down together.

Chapter 17

"It took some doing," Marc said into the baby monitor, "but we got it figured out. Over."

"It's not a walkie-talkie, and you're not a trucker," I said, exasperated. "And how much doing could it have taken? You started last night."

"Hey, next time *you* track down Damien. Whose name is Laura, by the way."

We were in the kitchen—everyone but Jessica—and I was getting the scoop on my lost-now-found sister. The three of them were unanimous in their dislike of screaming at Jessica's closed door, so Marc had picked up a set of baby monitors. He'd popped one into Jessica's room that morning, while she was out and the rest of us were conked.

She couldn't have minded—we didn't find the monitor in little pieces in the kitchen garbage, at least.

Wait a minute.

Laura?

"Satan's kid is named Laura?"

"Laura Goodman." Tina giggled.

"That's pretty dumb."

"Almost as ridiculous a name as Betsy for a vampire queen," Sinclair commented.

Was that a nasty comment or a nasty-nice comment? Was he getting over being mad? And why did I care so much? *He* was usually on *my* shit list.

I had to admit, I didn't much care for the role reversal. But what could I do? I had the distinct impression that apologizing for having sex with him would just make everything worse. And things were plenty bad enough, thanks. "So, what else did you guys find out?"

Plenty, as it turned out. Laura had been adopted about ten seconds after the Ant had dumped her, thank goodness, by the Goodmans, who settled with her in Farmington, where she grew up. Even better, Laura was a student at the U of M and had an apartment in Dinkytown. My mom could probably help me out a little there.

"It wasn't even very hard to find this stuff out," Marc added. He turned to Tina. "My review is tomorrow. Will you please come to work with me?"

She rolled her eyes and laughed again. "Oh, Marc."

"Well, I suppose it wouldn't have been," I said. I had great respect for Tina's sinister powers. Hey, trying to kill her could be seen as a compliment! A sad, lame compliment. "If there's someone out there Tina can't put the vamp mojo on, I haven't met them."

"Less mojo was needed than you would believe. Everyone was very open about . . . well, everything. The adoption and where she is now and what she's doing. We've even got her phone number."

"Well, good." I guess. That was good, right? Right! Time to regain control of this meeting. Assuming I'd ever had it. "So I guess we'll . . . what? Go see her? Track her down in the root of all evil—Dinkytown, is it? Tell her we're onto her, and she'd better not fulfill her destiny or we'll . . . what?"

"One thing at a time," Sinclair said. Since he was having very little to say these days, I was glad to hear him piping up. "We must find her first."

"Together?"

He speared me with his dark gaze. Which was as uncomfortable as it sounds. "You shouldn't speak to Satan's own by yourself. Of course, I will come with you."

"Of course." I smiled at him, but he didn't smile back.

"Meeting's over," Marc told the baby monitor. "Over."

Chapter 18

"She volunteers at the church," I said. "Oh. My. God! She *volunteers* at the *church*!"

"No matter how many times you say it out loud," Sinclair said, "it still seems to be true."

We'd been shadowing a group of kids—all girls in their late teens—for the last two hours. I wasn't sure which of them was my sister—there were three blondes, two brunettes, and even a strawberry blonde in the group. They'd gone from the U (my mom had most helpfully provided Laura's class schedule, breaking about twenty school regs in the process) to an apartment house in Dinkytown, and now they had all trooped into the local Presbyterian church.

"They're like a flock," Sinclair observed.

"That's just what girls do at that age." Heck, any age. "They travel in clumps. Like hair!"

"Charming."

We were in Sinclair's Passat. I know, I know . . . the king and queen of the vampires, tooling around in a blue Passat? He was keeping the really good cars—the convertible (a Mustang ironically a convertible), the Spider, the various other pretty cars that I didn't know the names of—under wraps for the time being.

Maybe he had hauled the good ones out before to impress me, and now that he was done with the mating dance, it was Passat time.

Ridiculous.

Right?

"I'm going in," I said. I waited for him to caution me, to warn me not to be heedless, to be careful, to insist I wait until the devil's spawn was in a place he could go, too.

Instead, I got, "That seems wise. We really must find out more about this girl."

"Well, so I'll go in. Wait here for me, okay?"

"Mmmm." He was squinting at the church again; I could have started disrobing, and he probably wouldn't have looked away.

"Hey, how come the devil's kid can go in a church and you can't?"

"Ask her," he suggested.

"I think I'll work up to that one," I replied and climbed out of the Passat to cross the street.

I opened the door and walked into the church, hoping Sinclair was noticing the awesome way I could do just that. Yay, the queen!

Argh, again, why did the queen *care*? Was the queen at heart a pathetic loser who could blow off a guy while he was all over her, but the minute he started ignoring her couldn't stop thinking about him? And why was the queen referring to herself in the third person?

But I had to admit, I'd been so focused on being mad at Sinclair for various sins against me, I'd sort of gotten used to him being around. Being concerned about me, always ready to take one for the team, that was Sinclair all the way. When he wasn't being sneaky and withholding.

Focus, idiot. Instead of the main part of the church, the part with the pews, I was in a dining area with tables and chairs all over. The gaggle of girls was in the far corner, chatting and giggling, and one of them—the tallest, the blondest, the prettiest—waved at me, said something to her friends, and walked over.

Too late, I realized I had no cover story. At all.

"Hi," she said, smiling. She was wearing a white button-down, crisp and spotless, with khaki pants and loafers. Beat up, ancient, cracked, yukky loafers; no socks. Her hair was long and fine, the blond strands looking like rough silk, and caught away from her face with a white headband. Her eyes were a perfect, clear blue, the exact color of the sky. Her skin was also irritatingly perfect, creamy with peach highlights, and not a freckle in sight. No makeup—she didn't need it.

And she was smiling so pleasantly at me, in her casual running-around clothes, that I instantly knew she was one of those beautiful girls who didn't know they were beautiful. It took all of my powers as the queen of the undead not to instantly hate her.

"Why are you and your friend following us?"

"Uh . . ." Because, as king and queen of the vampires, we feel that you—or one of your friends—as the devil's daughter (and worse, the Ant's daughter), should be stopped from ruling the world. Welcome to the family! Now get the fuck out. "We're . . . we're looking for Laura? Laura Goodman?"

"I'm Laura," she said, holding out a slim, pale hand for me to shake. I took it, being massively unsurprised. She was too tall (as tall as me!), too pretty, too perfect. And you know what they said about the devil taking a pleasing form. "What can I do for you?"

"Well . . . the thing is, I—"

"Laura!" One of her gaggle was calling over to us. "You coming? This dance isn't going to plan itself."

"Be right there," she called back, and turned back to me. "You were saying?"

"It's kind of a private thing. Do you have any time later tonight? Or tomorrow? Maybe we could have some coffee and talk?"

"Okay," she said, and she wasn't giving off scared vibes, which was good. Really trusting . . . or really scarily powerful with nothing to fear from the likes of me. "How about lunch tomorrow? Kahn's?"

"Ohhhh, I *love* Kahn's!" So we couldn't go there. If I couldn't eat the awesome garlic noodles with scallions and lamb, I wasn't going to watch someone else do it. "But lunch is bad for me."

"Well, I've got class tomorrow until four thirty . . ."

"How about Dunn Brothers, at five? Right around the corner?"

"All right, then." She shook my hand again. "It was nice to meet you . . ."

"Betsy."

"Right. See you tomorrow for coffee."

"Bye," I told my sister and watched her walk back to her friends.

"So she's this wretched evil beast who's fated to rule the world *and* she's a natural blonde. Just ridiculously pretty—hair, face, long thin legs, okay clothes, terrible shoes. And sweet as sugar, so far. When she turns into her horrible demon self it should be something to see . . .

"I didn't see much resemblance to the Ant or my dad, except for her being tall like me, and blond. But that's not too hard; we're in Minnesota, not Japan. I dunno. I'm having coffee with her tomorrow, trying to suss out her evilness . . . so I guess that's everything."

I clicked off the baby monitor and then remembered, so I turned it back on. "Almost forgot, I told Sinclair all about this, too. Sun's not going to be down all the way by five—I swear, vampires must have thought up daylight savings—but since it hasn't kicked in yet, he can't come. He didn't even seem to mind that he couldn't be there again. I guess he's still pretty pissed at me. Not that I blame him. Or you," I added hastily. "I can't seem to fix it with either one of you. And it's weird—it's bugging me that he's being so chilly and distant. And it's bugging me that it's bugging me. I can't apologize, and I can't pretend nothing happened. I guess . . . I guess I'll just focus on other stuff. Oh, my mom's having me over for supper the day after tomorrow, and she says you should come, too. If you want."

Silence.

I clicked the monitor off again and went up to bed.

Chapter 19

The devil's own—Laura Goodman, college girl about Dinkytown—breezed into Dunn Brothers at two minutes after five. She waved at me, paused to speak to the counter guy—who was slavering like a beast, I couldn't help noticing—and then came over to me.

"I'm so sorry I'm late," she gasped by way of greeting, shaking my hand again. "I'm really, really sorry. Have you been waiting long? I'm sorry."

"It's fine, Laura. By my watch you're right on time." She seemed so contrite, so sincere, I found myself rushing to reassure her. "Have a seat."

"Thanks. My cocoa's coming."

"Don't like the hard stuff, huh?" I asked, indicating my own doublechocolattespressowithextrafoam.

"Oh, I try not to drink caffeine after lunchtime," she replied. "I have to get up early in the morning for work."

"You've got a job, too?"

"Too? Oh, that's right." She smiled at me. It wasn't a grin, it wasn't a smirk, she didn't raise an eyebrow knowingly. It was just a nice smile. "You were following me half the night yesterday."

"Well, yeah," I admitted. "I guess it's no good pretending I wasn't."

"My father says liars are fated to believe their own lies, so it's probably good you're coming clean."

"Yeah . . . your father. Uh, listen about that . . ."

She leaned forward and took my hand in hers, then dropped it. "Gosh, your hand is cold! You should have another hot drink."

"Sorry. I have bad circulation."

"No, *I'm* sorry. I hope I didn't make you feel bad. I shouldn't have just blurted it out like that."

"Don't worry about it, Laura." She was too good to be true! Minnesota nice was one thing, but Laura was in a class by herself. "Listen . . ."

She leaned forward, perfect gorgeous face lighting up. "This is about my family, isn't it? My birth family." She paused, then added, "Sorry about interrupting."

I blinked in surprise. "How'd you know?"

"Well." The counter guy brought her a white coffee cup the size of my head, absolutely brimming with whipped cream and swirled with chocolate syrup. She smiled up at him and cupped the biggest cocoa in the world in her hands. "I was thinking about you last night, after you left. And you're tall, like me—in fact you're about an inch taller. My whole life, I've never met a woman taller than me. And you're blond, and we both have light-colored eyes . . . and you were so mysterious, but so nice . . . it just got me thinking."

"Oh, so you know you're—that you were adopted?"

"Yes, of course. Mama and Dad told me all about it, about how of all the babies in the world, they chose me." She was still smiling, clearly happy at the memory. "God brought me to them."

"Right." God. Uh-huh. "Well, I recently—like, this week—found out about you, and I did some detective work." With vampires. And a certain dark book bound in human skin. No, *not* chemistry. "And I tracked you down and—I don't know." I really *didn't* know where I was going with this. "I just wanted to meet you and then I guess . . ."

"You're my sister, right?"

"Half sister," I hastened to correct. I did not have a single drop of blood in common with the Ant *or* the devil.

Biologically, Laura was the Ant's own blood daughter, but without the interference of Satan, she never would have been born. It was enough to make me want to lunge for the Advil. "We have the same father." *And I'm so, so sorry about that, Laura.*

"Well, I'm just so pleased to meet you!" Impulsively, she leaned over further and flung her arms around my neck. I almost broke her arms before I realized she was hugging me, not attacking me. "I really, really am," she gushed. She was so close I could smell—vanilla? I'd smelled it before, natch, but being in a coffee shop, I'd assumed . . .

"Well, thanks," I said, gently extricating myself. "It's nice to meet you, too. Has anyone ever told you, you smell like cookies?"

"I use vanilla extract instead of perfume. It's cheap, and they don't test it on bunnies," she told me soberly.

"Huh. That's kind of clever, actually."

"People tell me that a lot." She sipped her cocoa and continued, oblivious of her whipped cream mustache. "I'm at the U on scholarship. Hmm, what else should I tell you? What do you want to know?"

"What are your folks like?"

She wiped the cream away with the back of her hand, then wiped her hand on the napkin. "They're wonderful. Dad is the minister at the Presbyterian church in Inver Grove—"

"Your dad's a *minister?*" I tried to dial back my total amazement and shock. I thought the *devil* was supposed to be in the details. "That's—really cool."

"Uh-huh. And Mama takes care of the house, and me. She's in school now, too! Now that I'm out of the house, she thought it would be a good time to finish up her nursing degree. We're students together at the U! Oh, you have to come over! They would love to meet you."

"That would be"—extremely weird; incredibly uncomfortable; horribly inconvenient right now—"great."

"What about you, Betsy? What do you do?"

As God was my witness, I had no idea what to say. I just couldn't blurt it all out to her. She was such a sweetheart, I didn't want to wreck her evening. Day. Month. Life. I resolved to take it one step at a time. "I'm—I run the—a—nightclub. A bar, actually. It's called Scratch, and I own it."

"You *own* it?"

"Well, it was left to me. By someone—" Who I staked. "Anyway, that's really my thing. I mean, that's what I do." That didn't sound suspicious, right?

"I'd love to see it sometime."

"Well, maybe I'll bring you by." Ha! The devil's daughter, checking out my undead nightclub. "You seem to be—I mean, you seem kind of together about all this."

I had to admit, this was so not what I expected. I expected threats, mustache-twirling death threats. Not a pleasant coffee in Dinkytown. The Book had warned me about her but hadn't mentioned what an innocent she'd be.

"Mama and Dad were very open about my background," she was explaining.

Not that open, honey. "Yeah?"

"And now that I'm out of the house, I was going to do some detective work of my own. I love Mama and Dad— of course!—but I was curious, you know? I had a lot of questions, but I didn't want to be disrespectful."

"Sure, I can totally get behind that."

She smiled at me gratefully. "Anyway, you just saved me a whole lot of work." She seemed so nice, so grateful, that I couldn't help returning her smile.

"It's just so nice to meet you."

"It's nice to meet you, too."

"I've always hoped for a sister."

"Actually, me, too. My folks split up when I was a kid—"

"I'm really sorry."

"Thanks. Anyway, I was pretty lonesome, and if it wasn't for my friend Jess, I don't know what—" Talking about Jessica made me feel like choking up. How could I tell Laura the truth . . . about anything? About what I was, how I'd been such an asshole, how she was supposed to be an asshole, too, and by the way, please don't take over the world. "We're kind of in a fight right now," I finished lamely.

"If I can ask . . . Betsy, I hope you're not offended . . ."

"Go ahead. I've butted into your life."

"Well . . . when your folks split up . . . was it because of me?"

"Oh no no no," I assured her. Then, "Well, maybe. A little. It wasn't your *fault*. I mean, you were just a fetus. But I guess when my mom had proof my dad was cheating . . . things sort of went downhill."

"Oh." She looked down at her lap. "I guess I don't really know how to feel about that. I'm sorry my birth father was faithless, but if he hadn't been . . ."

"Don't beat yourself up," I advised, in big sister mode. "Trust me, you'll screw up in your life enough without taking the blame for something that isn't your fault."

She looked up from her hands and smiled again. "I really—oh golly, who is *that*?"

I looked. Eric Sinclair, walking in . . . but not to order coffee, I bet. I realized the sun had fallen down while Laura and I were chatting.

"That's my—" I took another look at Laura's perfect beauty, the way she was goggling at Eric, remembered (like I could forget) his recent disinterest in me, and said it. "My boyfriend." Except that wasn't right, either. According to the Book, he was my consort, my husband, my king. I'd always felt just the opposite, that he wasn't anything to me—just another vampire in a city full of the darn things.

"He's your *boyfriend?*"

"Yep, that's my steady sweetie." I was digging myself quite the hole with my big fat mouth. But no matter how nice Laura was, I did not want the devil's daughter to know the king of the vampires was available. And vice versa.

"Elizabeth." Suddenly, Eric was right *there*, standing beside our little table by the window. I jumped and nearly threw my coffee into the window. He was holding a large foam cup with a straw sticking out of the cover, a cup that smelled like strawberries. The man was a nut for his smoothies.

"Hi, Sin—Eric. Ah, Eric, this is my sister, Laura. Laura, this is . . ."

He raised an eyebrow.

"Eric," I finally said. That wasn't a horrible weird awkward pause, was it?

"Charmed," he said.

"Hiya," she replied, dazzled. She shook his hand and gasped again. "Boy, you both have freezing cold hands! I guess you two are a pretty good match."

"Right!" I said. "That's what made us perfect for each other: clammy extremities. Laura and I were just catching up with each other."

"Pull up a chair," she invited. "Have you been dating long?"

Sinclair lifted the other eyebrow at "dating." I couldn't blame him. We had done quite a few things together, none of which could be classified as a date. "Six months," he said, sitting down. Then he paused, and added, "You smell like sugar cookies."

"She uses vanilla extract for perfume," I explained. "It's better for our animal friends,"

"Oh, yes, our animal friends." He barely seemed to notice my explanation. "My, my, Laura Goodman. I must say, that is a charming name for a charming young lady."

"Eric's old," I broke in. "Really really old."

"Er—really?" Laura asked. "Gosh, you don't look even out of your thirties."

"Tons of face-lifts. He's a surgical addict. I'm trying to get him help," I added defensively when they both gave me strange looks.

"I was just telling Betsy that my parents would love to meet her, and you must come, too."

"I would be delighted, Laura."

"Yeah," I said, watching the two of them stare at each other over foam cups. "That'd be swell."

Chapter 20

"I'm so sorry to bother you with this." It was the third time Alice had said it. "But I thought you ought to know."

"It's okay, Alice. It's not your fault. They're not animals, they're people. It's stupid to pretend they don't have human brains. I should have figured that out a long time before now."

"It's not your fault, Majesty. The fault lies with me. It's—"

"They should be recaptured and staked," Sinclair said, sounding bored.

"We've been over this," I snapped back.

"I suppose we have."

I didn't agree with his kill-all-Fiends mind-set, but his boredom with the subject wasn't much fun, either.

"It's not 'they,'" Alice supplied helpfully. "It's just one."

"Let me guess: George?"

"Yes, ma'am."

"Swell." The perfect end to a perfect night. The devil's daughter turned out to be sweet as cream, Sinclair gave off the distinct impression that he'd like to sample some of that cream, I was in hell, and George had gone on the lam again. "Just great."

"We'll find him again, ma'am."

"Okay, well, call me if he turns up."

"At once, Majesty."

"We'll keep our eyes peeled, not literally. Meanwhile, let's think of a better system to keep him. The others don't seem to want to get out, but George does, so let's figure out why and fix it so he can have what he wants here on the property. It's not the best plan in the world, but it's what we'll start with."

"Yes, Majesty."

"Swell," Sinclair said, and gave me a thin smile.

"What the hell are you doing following me around?" I griped. We'd driven back to the mansion in our cars, and I was bitching Eric out on the front lawn. "Like dealing with the spawn of Satan isn't touchy enough without you popping up like a jack-in-the-box with fangs."

"I wasn't following you," he pointed out coolly. "I was following her."

Nuts. I'd been afraid of that. "Why?"

"She is a fascinating creature. I had no sense of deceit from her, did you?"

"N—"

"All that potential power, that world-building power, wrapped up in a lovely package. A genuinely nice girl with no clue of the unholy power she could wield." He was practically rubbing his hands together. "To harness that power . . . if I could just—"

"We," I said. "If *we* could just."

"Yes, yes. Really, an engaging dilemma."

"That's just super," I said, managing to keep the acid bitterness out of my tone. Pretty much. "Look, one thing at a time. We've got to make nice with Jessica and find George."

"As you have made clear in the past," he reminded me, "those are your problems, not mine."

For a second I couldn't say anything; it felt like cold dread just—just grabbed my heart. Six months of pushing him away, and when I succeeded, I was sick about it. Which was sick.

And as upset as I was, I was also mad. Okay, I'd screwed up. He was an eighty-year-old dead guy. Like he'd never made a mistake in all that time?

When I finally found my voice, I went on the attack. Anything was better than feeling like the biggest loser in the world.

"*Listen,* jackass. Do you think you can stop sulking for five fucking minutes and *help me?* Is that too fucking much to ask? If you won't admit you're mad, then you'd better be on board with the dark evil stuff like usual. You can't have it both ways."

He looked down at me, totally unmoved. "You . . . would . . . be . . . *amazed* at what I can have." Then he turned away.

I grabbed his sleeve and tried to pull him back. "Don't walk away from me, you—"

"Did you hear something?" he asked, shaking free of me with no trouble at all. "There's—" Then he was gone, knocked a good six feet sideways by something.

"Eric!" I called, like every useless movie heroine in the history of cinema. I charged over to grab whatever had tackled him. "Let go!" *And thanks!*

I leaned forward to seize whatever by the back of the neck—assuming it had a back of a neck—when suddenly it got off Sinclair and stood.

And stood. And stood. It was tall, even slumped over.

Long dirty clots of hair hung in its face, and its clothing—filthy jeans and a T-shirt of no definable color—was in rags. Bare feet. Filthy toes.

"George!" I gasped.

"How completely fabulous," Sinclair said, getting up off the ground and brushing himself off. There were leaves in his hair, but *I* wasn't going to tell him. "I assume he followed us. Or tracked you."

"Tracked *me?*"

"They are uncommonly attached to you, in case you've forgotten their devotion when they killed Nostro," he snorted, as if I *could* forget.

"Aw, shaddup. George, you were very very bad to run away from Alice." I shook my finger under his nose. It was a little disconcerting the way he followed my finger with his muddy gaze. "Very bad! But you were very good to stomp Sinclair when he was being a dick, so I think we'll call this a wash."

"What?" Sinclair scowled. "How can you say—"

"Pipe down, ass hat. You know what, George? Let's call Alice and have her come get you. Good, good Fiend!"

"No, no, no," Sinclair began. At least he was evincing some interest again—interest that didn't threaten the hell out of me.

"And while we're waiting, you can have a shower."

"Elizabeth, I must protest."

"Really?"

"Yes."

"Hate the idea, do you?"

"Completely."

"Good enough." I took George's cold, grimy hand, and he followed me.

Chapter 21

$\mathcal{I}$ didn't dare bring him into the main part of the house—Jessica and Marc were probably around, and I didn't quite trust George enough to just let him go like that movie *Born Free*. So I brought him through one of the basement doors, helped him strip, and stuck him under the shower we had down there.

He seemed to like it, creepy darkened basement notwithstanding, first standing like a hairy lump and then stretching a bit under the beating warm water. I dared leave him for just a moment, superspeeding my way through the house to grab some of Marc's clothes. Marc, shaving, didn't hear me or see me, and I'd explain later.

George was shaking his head under the spray so his

long strands flew when I got back to the basement, and I let him enjoy the shower for another ten minutes. I almost couldn't bear to turn it off; seeing him clean and almost happy gave me a glimpse of the man he once had been.

Not a bad-looking one, either, under all the mud. Tall and thin, with long arms and legs that were sleekly muscled, and a broad back and a *great,* tight butt. Very pale, of course, but a clean, open-looking face with thin lips. He looked like a swimmer, in fact, all gangly limbs and big feet. And big, uh, other things, but I was trying to stay clinical.

"So, why'd you come after me?" I asked.

No answer, big surprise.

"It's creepy," I added, "but kind of cute. You must have thought I was in danger from Sinclair." I snickered, remembering seeing Sinclair practically knocked out of his loafers on the front lawn. "Well, Alice is on her way, so you'll be back home soon."

When the water started to get chilly, I shut it off and draped George in a humungous beach towel. Impersonal as a nurse, I briskly dried him off, helped him get dressed in a set of Marc's scrubs, then combed out his long hair. Under the light, it was past his shoulders—which was weird, vampires couldn't grow their hair—and brown with gold highlights. It must have been long when he'd died. What had he been? Rock drummer? Motorcycle racer?

"There now!" I said, stepping back to admire him. "You look great. If you can just resist rolling around in the mud, you could almost pass for an ordinary creature of the night."

"Majesty?" I could hear Alice calling me—I must not have heard her car over the sound of the shower. "The king said you were down here."

"Yeah, come on down, Alice." She tentatively crept down the stairs, obviously ready to be yelled at. It was tough work reminding some of these guys that I wasn't Nostro with red highlights. "Look who I found! Doesn't he look great?"

She stared. "George?"

"In the undead flesh." I reached up—way up—and tousled his hair. "He must have followed me home. Or picked up my scent and followed that. You should have seen him tackle Sinclair. It was great! Disrespectful," I added with mock severity, "but great."

"Again, Majesty, I'm so s—"

"Alice, for crying out loud. You've got your hands full, I know that. In fact, I should get you some help." What other vampire could I trust with such a tedious but important, job? Maybe I'd find one at Scratch.

"He looks"—she was circling around him, a good trick since she had to actually go through the shower to do it—"different. It's not just being clean. He's been clean before."

"It's the scrubs," I decided. "They make him look smarter."

"Nooooo, with all respect, I don't think that's it." She looked at George, then me, then George. I waited to hear her theory. Alice looked like a demure fifteen-year-old in her plaid skirts and headbands, but she was really, like, fifty years old. And no dummy, either. "Ah, well."

That was her big theory?

"We've taken up quite enough of your evening, Majesty. Come on, George." Alice put her hand out and clutched his forearm, which he yanked back so quickly she almost fell into the shower. He didn't growl at her, but he showed his teeth.

"Uh-oh," she murmured.

"Maybe he wants to stay here with me," I said, a little surprised.

"I don't think it's a maybe. Perhaps if you helped me get him out to the car . . ."

"You know what? Let him stay."

"Majesty, you live in the city. I'm not sure that's wise. He might—"

"He's had plenty of chances to pounce—heck, he didn't do anything to Sinclair except knock him out of the way. I know! I'll let him feed on me and then he can just stay in the basement for a couple of nights."

"*You'll* let him feed?"

I didn't take offense at Alice's reaction. It was well-known that I wasn't the biggest pro–blood giver among vampires. Except with Sinclair, the whole thing kind of squicked me out.

Well, Sinclair was over! The past! I was going forward, not back. And while I was at it, the hell with Jessica, too. I had two new friends: the devil's daughter and George the Fiend.

It sounded so ridiculous I didn't dare dwell on it; instead I chomped on my own wrist until my sluggish blood started to flow, and held my arm out to George.

"Thish should do it," I slurred. *My life isn't horrible and weird. My life isn't horrible and weird. My life—*

"I must admit," Alice commented, her red hair seeming to glow against the gloomy basement bricks, "when I rose this evening, I hadn't foreseen any of tonight's events."

"Thtick with me, bay-bee." George had grasped my wrist, lapped up the blood, and was now sucking like a kid with a Tootsie Pop. "Ith a new thrill every minute."

Alice reluctantly left, I managed to get my arm back, and then I made George a nest in one of the empty basement rooms—one of the inner windowless ones—with a bunch of clean towels. I went upstairs to find a pillow, saw the usual unrelieved darkness outside was now a dark gray, and hurried back down, hauling a wool blanket out of one of the linen closets on the way. George was already stretched out on the towels, sound asleep.

I left him the pillow, locked the door—compassion was one thing, carelessness something else—and went up to my room.

It had been an unnatural night, that was for sure. Good in some ways—bad in others, and, ultimately, challenging.

Chapter 22

". . . So that's the really bizarro thing," I told the baby monitor. "She's not this incredibly evil creature out to rule the world. She's a perfectly nice college kid. An education major, for God's sake! She wants to teach kindergarten when she grows up. If you cut her, she'd probably bleed maple syrup.

"So anyway, on the one hand that's a relief, but on the other, I can't just let her run around being unconsciously evil. I guess I better tell her. One of these days. And how do you tell someone that their mom is the devil? It would have been hard enough to tell her the *Ant* was her mom.

"And let's not forget what the Book told me. The devil's supposed to show up. She's—I guess it's a she—she's supposed to show up to Laura, poor thing, and to me. 'In all the raiments of the dark,' whatever that means. So I can't dick around with warning Laura. Right?"

Silence. Was Jess even listening to her baby monitor? I had no way of knowing. Her car was in the garage, but who really knew?

"Right," I finished. "Well, so that's what's been going on. That and there's a Fiend living in the basement, so don't go down there during the day. In fact, don't go down there altogether. Listen, if you want to meet Laura, just let me know. She's really a sweetheart. She's having me over for supper pretty soon. And Sinclair, unfortunately, but I'll worry about that later. Well, 'bye."

I snapped the monitor off and just sat at the kitchen counter for a minute, thinking. Tina came in and nodded respectfully; I sort of waved at her and kept with the pondering.

Jessica was still mad . . . and worse, scared. She'd been mad before, plenty of times, but she'd never hidden herself away for days (nights) at a time. Her method was normally to tell me at length, loudly, how and where I'd fucked up, repeat as needed.

My sister was running around the campus of the University of Minnesota, totally unaware she was going to try to take over the world one of these days. Sinclair was still giving me frostbite every time he looked at me. The Ant was still pregnant. Only Marc seemed unchanged by it all and, frankly, with his work schedule, he had never been around all that much to begin with.

My cat Giselle walked into the kitchen, ignored both of us, and headed to her bowl. I didn't bother trying to pet or cuddle her. Giselle and I had a strict working relationship. I worked to feed her, and she worked on ignoring me. Plus, in a house this big, days would go by when I didn't see her. I made sure she had food and fresh water, and she ate and drank and did her own thing.

Well, at least someone else's life was unchanged.

"Everything sucks," I announced. "Again."

"I'm sorry to hear that, Your Majesty." Tina glanced up from *Outdoor Life*. She was a gun nut, that one. "I'm sure you'll find a way to make it all right again."

"All right *again*? Tina, when has it ever been all right?"

"A poor choice of words," she admitted, turning a page. Reading upside down, I could see the title of the article: "Tracking Antelope in Big Sky Country."

"And as nutty as everything is, I've got the nagging feeling I'm forgetting something." I thought and thought. "What the hell is it?" Monique? Dead. Sister? Friend. Scratch? Still in the red. But that reminded me—Monique had hired a bunch of pimply faced vampire killers last summer. To be honest, once they'd stopped trying to cut my head off, I'd sort of forgotten about them. "What are the Blade Warriors up to these days?"

"Jon is still at his parents' farm, Wild Bill is out of town at the SciFiConBiTriCon, and I have no idea what the others are doing. Frankly," she admitted, "once they stopped trying to stake us, I instantly lost interest in their activities."

I could relate. "Except for Ani," I said slyly.

Tina smiled. "Well. We had to go our separate ways, but she was a very charming girl."

"Right. Charming. We *are* talking about the girl who has more knives than shirts, right? Don't answer. Okay, so it's not that. What *is* it?"

"Well, you were planning to shop for new shoes for Andrea and Daniel's wedding," she pointed out. "With all the goings on, perhaps you haven't had—"

"Andrea and Daniel's wedding!" I nearly shouted, then rested my forehead on the cool marble counter. "Aw, fuck a duck."

"I take it you've remembered what you had forgotten?"

"When is it?" I asked hollowly.

"Halloween. A week from tomorrow."

"Swell." Jessica was supposed to help me shop. Maybe I'd turn on the baby monitor and remind her. No, she knew. Unlike me, she had a great memory. She was just ignoring it. Not that I could blame her, but the cold shoulder *was* getting old.

"Aha!"

"I tremble to ask."

"I'll ask my sister to go shopping! You know, one of the few people on the planet who don't think I'm scum."

"Majesty—"

"Don't bother, Tina. And don't mind me. I'm sort of neck deep in self-pity right now."

She smiled sympathetically. "I'm sure you'll work everything out. Who could resist you for long, my queen?"

"Thanks. That's a little creepy, but thanks. I—"

Suddenly, so fast I could barely follow it, Tina's hand dropped to the knife block, she pulled out a wicked long butcher knife, and whipped it underhand toward me in one smooth motion. I squeaked and got ready to duck (to try to duck), when I realized she hadn't been aiming at me.

George the Fiend blinked at us from the kitchen doorway, a knife sticking out of his chest.

"Damn," she swore, getting up. "Majesty, get back. I'll—"

"You'll stop throwing sharp things at his heart, that's what you'll do!" I leapt up and went to George, who didn't seem especially fazed. "He's okay, Tina, he's not here to hurt us. Jeez, good thing it's not a wooden stake."

"I never even heard him approach, blast it." Tina wasn't this upset when she called Sinclair on keeping secrets about my sis. "I was trying to buy time for you to get away. I would have found something suitable in another few seconds."

"That's comforting." Okay, it wasn't, but what else was I supposed to say? "Good work. Except don't throw knives at him anymore."

Tina's dark eyes were practically bulging. "My queen, what is he doing in our kitchen?"

"He must have gotten out of the basement. Stop me if you've heard this before, but George is the Houdini of feral vampires. I'm gonna have to get him a straitjacket or something. And a cowbell." I patted him soothingly, then grasped the handle of the knife, gritted my teeth, and pulled. It stuck to his breastbone for half a second, then slid out. Yecccch!

George the Fiend hummed a little but otherwise stood still for it. He didn't bleed.

"My goodness," Tina goggled. "He didn't even notice!"

"Yeah, he's the Fiend you love to stab. Poor George, does it hurt? Of course it doesn't hurt. You'd probably be screaming like a third-grade girl if it hurt. Listen, you're supposed to *stay* in the *basement.*"

"He's not bleeding," she said, coming over to inspect the stab wound.

"Well, he's dead."

"We do bleed," she reminded me. "Not much compared to a living, breathing human, but we do." She bent forward . . . then jerked back as George growled at her.

"Better not," I said. "I think he only likes me. And Alice. But then, she feeds him." And so did I, I remembered suddenly. I'd let them drink my blood the night we killed Nostro . . . and again last night.

"He's dangerous," Tina nagged.

"Yeah, yeah, thanks for the update. Listen, they're Fiends because Nostro let them rise but not feed, right?"

"Yes."

"Well. I *have* let them feed. I mean, Alice feeds them buckets of blood from the butcher, but it's not live blood. They're the only vampires that can subsist on—what would you call it? Dead blood? Unfresh blood? But maybe that's what keeps them like animals. I fed George last night, and here he's walking around and—well, being creepy, but look! He's not crawling. He's *walking*. He stood in the shower last night, too," I remembered.

"I see where you're going with this."

"Good, because I don't have a clue . . . I was just thinking out loud."

I looked at his chest again. "See, he's not bleeding, not like you or I would. Maybe he has to—I dunno—build up? Maybe I can cure him!"

175

"And maybe you should think this over some more before . . . oh, Majesty," she scolded as I chomped on my own wrist again. "As you would say, this is so totally the opposite of thinking this over."

"Where's your spirit of adventure?"

"It wore off during World War Two," she replied dryly. Meanwhile, George was obligingly sucking on my wrist, still humming.

"That almost sounds . . . familiar."

"It's the Beastie Boys! 'Brass Monkey'!"

"Is that good?"

"Dunno, but it's a song. He's standing, and he knows rap songs." It was working! I would cure him, I'd cure them all. And Laura wouldn't take over the world. And Sinclair would forgive me and want to sleep with me again. And Jessica would stop being mad and scared and go shopping with me. Everything was working out great!

"Isn't tomorrow your stepmother's baby shower?" Tina asked, and I instantly sank back into a funk.

Chapter 23

". . . And then I graduated valedictorian at my school and got to give the speech to all the kids, and then I got a job volunteering at Goodwill, in addition to my jobs at Target and SuperAmerica, while I waited to start at the U in the fall."

I stifled a yawn and shifted the phone to my other ear. If you'd ever told me the devil's daughter would be nice, but dull . . . "Yeah, then what happened?"

"Well, that's about it. I mean, I'm still in school. Nothing much has happened to me yet."

Give it time, sweetie.

"What about you, what have you been doing? You're— what? Twenty-five?"

I laughed. "Actually, I turned thirty in April. And I've had kind of a checkered career. Model, secretary, waitress . . ."

"And right now you own a nightclub?"

"Right now, yeah." I'd just looked over the books the other night, in fact. We were definitely in the red—I was shocked at the price of booze, not to mention utilities—but so far I had been able to borrow from Peter to pay Paul. Without Jessica's help, I couldn't much longer. But it was hard enough to ask her for a loan when she *wasn't* pissed and terrified. "I guess we'll see how that goes."

"So, tell me about my birth mother and father."

That was the *last* thing I wanted to do. I downed my hot milk in a hurry and tried not to drop the phone. She'd called me about a minute after I'd woken up that afternoon. Three thirty in the afternoon, yippee! A new record. Maybe someday I'd manage to wake at lunchtime. "Uh, well . . . gee, so much to tell. Where to start. Ah . . ."

"Do you think I could meet them sometime? I wouldn't want to push my way into their lives. I understand they gave me up because it was what they thought was best for me. I wouldn't want to intrude or make them uncomfortable in any way."

"Don't forget, Dad didn't even know you existed until after you were adopted." Why had I said that? Did I want her to like Dad? Maybe I was so dreading telling her about the devil, I wanted her to have something nice to hold on to.

"That's true, Betsy. And I know my mother was alone . . . poor thing, she must have been so worried when she found out. No one to turn to . . . maybe her minister was able to counsel her."

Her minister, her bookie, whatever. "Yeah, the . . . poor thing." Suddenly, a wonderful (or terrible) idea came to me. "Listen! Do you want to meet them both? This afternoon?" The shower started in . . . I checked my watch. Twenty minutes. Well, we'd be fashionably late.

Laura's happy squeal was answer enough.

"She's pregnant again?" Laura asked, staring at the Ant's too-big-for-two-people house. "At her age?"

"She's not that old, remember." I checked my lipstick in the mirror. Next to Laura's breathtaking, fresh beauty, I don't know why I bothered.

She looked wonderful; her hair was in two golden braids today, the ends brushing the tops of her breasts, her bangs perfectly level with her eyebrows. She was wearing a clean white blouse (she must have a closet full of them) and a navy A-line skirt. No panty hose, and sensible black flats. Isaac Michener, good. The Target collection, bad. She looked like an extra on *Touched by an Angel*. And I felt like a before on *Nip/Tuck.*

"I'm so excited!"

"Oh, she will be, too," I lied. "Let's go."

We knocked politely but, since it was a party, opened the massive front door and went right in. The driveway was packed with cars, and I could hear the gabble of voices off to the right.

The Ant came hurrying out to greet us, the smile vanishing when she saw it was me. She glanced over my shoulder to the windows on either side of the door, confirming the sun was still up, looked back at me, looked out the window.

"Surprise!" I burbled.

"Congratulations," Laura said.

The Ant swallowed her tongue and forced a grimace that I suppose was technically a smile. "Thank you for coming," she managed. "Betsy, you know where to hang up your coats."

Laura handed me her knee-length mustard-colored trench coat. (I know it sounds awful, but on her, it worked. She probably could have worn the kitchen curtains and it would have worked.) I slung it into the hall closet.

"Gifts . . . gifts can go in the living room. There's a table."

"We didn't bring a present," I informed her gleefully. "Just our bad old selves."

"We have a gift," Laura corrected me. Now that I'd relieved her of her coat, I saw she was holding a small box of Tiffany blue, with the standard white ribbon.

Relief washed over the Ant's face; I could almost hear her thought: Not a total disaster after all! She practically snatched the present out of Laura's hand and ripped the ribbon off. Inside was a sterling silver baby spoon.

"Why, this is—it's very nice. Thank you, er—"

"Laura Goodman, ma'am. I'm a friend of Betsy's."

"Well, you might as well come in and have some cake," she almost snapped. To Laura, she added warmly, "So nice *you* could come."

Big surprise, Laura the Great had won over the second most evil creature in the universe. And where'd the present come from? She was a college student on scholarship; I doubted she kept a closetful of Tiffany baby gifts around.

Sixteen thousand years later, it was almost seven o'clock, and guests were pulling on their coats. Laura and the Ant were chatting like old pals—Laura seemed to think everything about her birth mother, from the bleached hair to the fuzzy pastel sweater to the knockoff pumps—was just swell. Me, I was ready to bite everybody in the room just for the relief of the screams. It was the usual collection of wannabe socialites and poseurs. Believe me, a bite on the neck would doing every one of them a favor. The fact that they all didn't recognize me—or pretended not to—was one of the nicest things that had happened all week.

"Come by anytime," the Ant told the devil's daughter. She didn't say anything to me, but her look spoke volumes.

"That was *great*!" Laura yammered on the way back to the car. "Wow, what a gorgeous house! And she's so nice! And pretty, don't you think she's pretty? I wish I could have told her the truth—I feel so bad about lying. And to a pregnant lady!"

"You didn't lie," I said, wondering why there was never a pack of feral vampires around when you needed them. "We *are* friends. Just ones who haven't known each other very long."

"Oh, Betsy." She slung an arm across my shoulders and gave me a one-armed hug. "You're the greatest. Thank you so much for bringing me here today."

"Umf," I said, or something close to it. "Listen, can I ask you something?"

"Sure. Anything."

"How'd you have a present all ready to go?"

"Oh, I bought that a long time ago," she explained with awe-inspiring (yet slightly nauseating) earnestness. "I always knew I'd meet my birth mother someday. The spoon was actually for *me*—you know, like a gag gift. But it works even better to give it to my future brother or sister. Just think, I was an only child my whole life, and now I'll have two siblings!"

"That's super," I said. I'd been half-hoping for an evil explanation but was yet again disappointed.

"Well, I have homework to do, so can I trouble you to take me back to my apartment?"

"Why? It's still early." And I had nothing to do. No one to go home to. Tina had given George a dozen balls of yarn—balls of yarn—and he was busy unrolling them and rerolling them when I left. Tina had stayed behind, amused, to watch him (at a prudent distance). Marc had work, as usual. Jessica was gone—her car was, anyway. Sinclair was somewhere, but I wasn't about to go looking for another dose of chill nasty.

"Gosh, Betsy, I don't know . . ."

"Oh, come on. You're not at the minister's house anymore, Laura, time to let your hair down. Literally—those braids are a little 2002. Or 1802. I know! We'll go to the Pour House. We can drink daiquiris, talk about boys, go crazy."

"I can't, Betsy."

"Pleeeeease?" I wheedled.

"I mean I really can't. I'm not twenty-one. I'm not allowed to drink."

"Oh, that." I pushed away federal law with a wave of my hand. "I can get you in, don't worry about that." One peek at my mold-colored eyes, and no bouncer would be able to resist.

"No, Betsy," she said as firmly as I'd ever heard. "It's against the law."

"Fine, fine." I sighed, then brightened. "I know! Let's go shopping! The mall will be open for another couple of hours. I've got a wedding to go to; we can look for an outfit and shoes and stuff."

"I can't," she said apologetically. "I don't have any money. And it wouldn't be right to—"

"That's okay, I—" Didn't have any money, either. Normally Jess would go with me, and she'd either pick up the tab outright or we'd work out a deal—I'd put in a few days at The Foot, her nonprofit org, in return for a cashmere sweater or pair of sandals. "Uh . . . hmm . . ."

"Maybe we should call it a night."

"Yeah, okay." I was disappointed at the sorry state of affairs my life had come to, but there was no use taking it out on Laura.

Not to mention, she was a nice kid and all, but she was no substitute for my friend. Or Sinclair. I'd been wrong to use her as a distraction.

"Wait!" I said, almost driving into a streetlight. "I've got it! We'll go to Scratch."

"Your club?" she asked doubtfully.

"Yeah. And I won't sell you a drop of booze, I promise. We'll just check it out, and then I'll take you home." What recently learned lesson about how you couldn't swap friends like baseball cards?

"Well . . ." She was weakening! Either my fiendish undead powers of persuasion were working on her, or she had any kid's curiosity about how the inside of a bar looked. "Maybe just a quick look . . ."

"Yippee!" I called, and wrenched the wheel to the left.

"Wow," Laura goggled. "It's in here? It's so nice!"

"Here" was a well-kept brownstone; in fact, the place looked just like somebody's home. Now that I knew it was a vampire bar, I knew why: the more innocuous the surroundings, the better.

"I'll just park out front," I said, and set the emergency brake. Nobody was going to tow it in *this* neighborhood.

I walked in, Laura right on my heels, and was a little bummed to see how dead the place was. Of course, it was early—only about seven thirty—but still. Except for a couple of vampire waitresses, and Slight Overbite manning the bar, the place was deserted.

"How's business?" I half-joked when Slight Overbite left the bar to greet us.

"The same, Ma—"

"This is my sister, Laura," I interrupted. "You can just call her Laura. Laura, this is—" It occurred to me that I'd forgotten his name again. "This is the guy who looks after the bar for me when I'm not here."

"Klaus, ma'am." He bent over her little white hand, and when he looked up at her from that position, an alarming amount of the whites of his eyes showed. It was like looking into the face of a corpse. "Charmed."

Laura, thank God, didn't notice Klaus's extreme yukkiness. And, even better, seemed immune to his charm. Of course, Klaus wasn't all *that* charming, but still . . . "Hi there," she said, shaking his hand. "It's real nice to meet you."

I practically jerked her away from Slight Overbite, who was looking as though all his Christmas wishes were coming true at once. What had I been thinking? Bringing my sweet little sister to a bar run by vampires? Sure, I was the head bloodsucker, and she wasn't in any danger, but still. Exposing her to Klaus and the sullen waitstaff . . . I was out of my mind.

"Ah, Laura."

I spun around, and there was Sinclair, looming over us like a big black bird of prey. "Elizabeth," he said, obviously noticing me for the first time. At least he'd remembered my name.

"Hi again," Laura said, dazzled. And who could blame her? That hair, those eyes, those shoulders . . . yum. To think that it had all been mine, and I'd thrown it away by . . . uh . . . sleeping with it. I guess.

"What are you two doing here?" he asked, a shade of disapproval in his deep voice. I knew "you two" meant "Laura." I wasn't about to explain that desperation and loneliness had driven me to yet another boneheaded move. So I did what I always do:

"Why don't you mind your own fucking business for *once?*" I snapped. "If I want to take my sister to my place of business, that's my own damned business and not any of your business." Was I overusing the word *business?* Fuck it. "So mind your own business."

"Betsy!" Laura gasped.

"Quiet, you." Lectures from the spawn of Satan/Ms. Goody-goody 2005 I *so* did not need.

"It's inappropriate for her to be here, and you know it. What were you thinking?"

"That you should mind your own business?" *And stop following my sister?*

"I think I'd like to go home now," Laura said primly.

I opened my mouth, but Sinclair beat me to the punch. "Allow me to see you home, Laura," he said, proffering his arm for her to take.

"Oh. Well . . ." She glanced at me—for approval or help,

I wasn't sure—and I shrugged. "All right, then. That's very kind of you."

"It's my great pleasure."

They walked out.

That was it. My life was now officially horrible. Worse than horrible. I'd be tempted to jump off a cliff, except I knew I'd survive it.

"Give me some Dewar's," I told Klaus.

"I can't," he replied smugly. "You haven't paid the liquor bill, and we're out."

Of course we were.

Depressed beyond all measure, I drove home.

Chapter 24

Before I could drive myself through a plate glass window, my cell phone rang. Jessica? I clawed it out of my purse. "Hello? Jess? Hello?"

"Hi, Betsy. It's me, Nick. Berry," he added, like I could forget. Nick was a Minneapolis cop.

"Oh, hey." I was disappointed but worked on not showing it. "Who's dead now?" I joked.

"Several people, but that's not why I'm calling. Listen, I haven't seen your new digs, and I just got off. I thought I'd come over and say hi."

"Oh. Look, I'm glad to have you over, Nick, but why now?"

"Well . . ." I heard an odd sound in the background and

realized he was chewing on a Milky Way. Nick abhorred donuts. "This is going to sound a little out there, but I haven't been able to get you out of my mind lately. I mean, you gotta admit, that whole thing last spring where you almost died and they had a fake funeral and all—"

"Yeah, last spring was a real laugh riot."

"And then this summer with all the dead bodies—I guess the killer moved on, because there hasn't been one like it in about three months—but you were sort of in the middle of that, too—and . . . I don't know. I just thought it'd be fun to stop by, catch up."

"Well, sure." Come on into my parlor, big boy. Actually, the last thing I wanted was the cop who had known me in life nosing around in Vampire Central after my death, but I couldn't think of a way to say no without arousing his suspicions. "I'm on my way there now. I'm guessing there's no need to give you the address, seeing as how you're the man and all."

"See you in twenty," he confirmed.

I hurried into the mansion to straighten up but realized Jessica's corps of home helpers (the cook, the gardener, the garage guy, the downstairs guy, the upstairs lady, the plant lady) was way ahead of me. The place was immaculate and freshly vacuumed. Marc's car was gone, but Jessica's was in the garage, so I darted up the stairs and knocked on her door.

"Jess? Detective Nick is coming over to play Welcome Wagon, which isn't much good in the way of timing, but seriously, when *is* the best time for a cop to come over? When you're not a vampire," I answered myself. "Anyway, if you want to come down, we'll be in"—Where? Where was a vampire-free zone?—"one of the parlors. I think."

I went to the basement and found Tina sitting a prudent distance away from George, scribbling notes, while he crocheted an endless chain in sunshine yellow. He'd churned out about thirty feet so far and didn't look up when I shrieked.

"You gave him a hook?" I could hear a car pulling in and didn't wait around for Tina's answer. At least George was occupied.

Nick was waiting at the door, and I played ditz and "forgot" to give him a tour. We ended up shooting the breeze in the small sitting room just off the front hall.

"This place is amazing," he said, staring. As always, he was easy on the eyes. My height, blond, broad-shouldered, tan. Ooooh, a tan! It was really great to see someone with real color in their cheeks. "You and Jessica are really moving up in the world."

"Ha!" I replied. "Jess pays for the whole thing."

"Well, yeah." He grinned boyishly. "I figured. Have you

found a job yet? Not that you need one, I guess . . ." He gestured to the room.

I *didn't* need one since I had the whole queen thing going, but I wasn't telling him that. Likewise, I didn't dare tell him about Scratch. I couldn't prove to a live person that I legally owned it. I sure didn't need a cop snooping into it.

Nick wasn't just any cop. He'd known me in life but, worse, had fallen under my vampiric spell after I died. Sinclair had ended up making Nick forget quite a bit from last spring. But it was a worrisome thing sometimes; we honestly didn't know what he remembered or if Sinclair's mojo would wear off.

"You look great," I said, changing the subject. "You're so tan! Where'd you go?"

"I just got back from Grand Cayman. Me and a bunch of the other guys saved up for about a year and a half. It's really not that expensive if you go in a group. Actually, that's sort of why I'm here."

"I can't go to Grand Cayman with you," I joked. I wasn't up to pushing the new sunshine allowances.

"No, no." Of course not. Why would a healthy red-blooded male want to date a corpse with badly polished toes? "One of the guys was looking for a new place to go to an AA meeting, and I knew from my brother that they had a good group at the Thunderbird—on 494? Anyway—"

"You were there the night I went," I said with a sinking feeling. It was definitely weird the way Nick kept stumbling back into my life. What were the chances?

"Well . . . yeah. And it's none of my business at all . . ."

"One of the *A*s stands for *Anonymous,*" I pointed out.

"Yeah, I know. My brother did the twelve steps a couple years ago. I just—I guess I was surprised to see you there," he finished lamely.

He was surprised! Was my luck *ever* going to take a turn for the better? "Well, it's nothing I like to talk about," I said, sort of telling the truth.

"Sure, sure, sure," he said quickly. "I understand. I just wanted you to know . . . well, sometimes it's a hard thing to talk about. It's like nobody else can possibly get it, right?"

"Right," I said, on surer ground.

"So I just wanted you to know that if you ever wanted to, you know, just talk . . ." He trailed off and smiled at me, which made the cute laugh lines in the corner of his eyes crinkle in a friendly way.

I nearly wept; it was beyond wonderful to have someone be nice to me, to be concerned with my problems. Well, that wasn't fair; Laura was nice, and Jessica *had* been concerned until I'd hurt her. It wasn't Laura's fault Sinclair was taken with her. What guy wouldn't be? And it wasn't Sinclair's fault he'd decided I'd given off negative vibes one too many times.

Poor Nick didn't have a clue, but he cared. That counted for a lot.

"That's so sweet of you. I really appreciate it." We'd been sitting next to each other on the little peach-colored love seat, and he was inching closer to me. Maybe he had an itch. "And I promise I'll keep it in mind. But I really don't want to talk about my dumb problems right now." My incredibly lame, stupid, dumb problems.

"I just—wanted you to know," he breathed, and then he kissed me.

Oh, yay! No, boo. No, yay! I let him go for a few seconds, quite enjoying the feeling of a warm mouth on my cool one. I could hear his pulse thundering in my ears. He smelled like chocolate and cotton.

It was actually kind of nice. He liked me. He'd always liked me. Of course, since I'd died he'd found me way more attractive, but I tried not to take advantage of it. Except for that one time. Which Nick didn't remember. I was pretty sure. But anyway . . . not taking advantage of innocent policeman.

Although without much difficulty I could. He was so nice, so great-looking, so earnest—and as a cop, he'd come in *real* handy. I could—I could—

Take him.

I could get rid of this annoying thirst for the moment, that's what I could do. I could—

What are you waiting for?

—get a little warmth, a little happiness, be needed, be touched, be wanted.

It would be so easy.

I jerked away, actually throwing Nick to the floor. It *would* be easy. Real damn easy. Which is why I couldn't do it.

Is that why I read the Book . . . to learn how to be an asshole vampire? Is that what I learned from hurting Jessica—take what I wanted when I could get it? Is that how my mom raised me? Is that the kind of queen of the dead I wanted to be?

"Jeez, I'm so sorry," Nick said from the floor, apparently overlooking the fact that I'd thrown him on his ass. His face was red with blushes. "I'm really sorry, Betsy."

"No, no, it's my fault!" I was shouting to hear myself over his pulse, which alarmed him. I lowered my voice. "Sorry. It's my fault." It really was. Nick had no idea why he found me so appealing. God knew it was a mystery to me most times, too. "Sorry again. You'd better go." I hauled him to his feet and showed him the door, over his protests and apologies. "Thanks for stopping by. Great to catch up! 'Bye."

I shut the door and leaned against it with my eyes closed. I could still hear his pulse, though that was probably my imagination.

It had been a near thing.

"Is your date over already?"

My eyes popped open. Sinclair was standing on the left side of the entryway; he'd obviously come through the back.

"That was—"

"I know."

"He thinks—"

"I know."

"But he's going now, I—"

"Yes, I imagine you took care of it. Good work," he added distantly.

"It wasn't—"

"I understand. The last thing you—we—need is a police officer nosing about. And the quickest way to get rid of him—" Sinclair shrugged. "Well, you did what you had to do."

"Eric—"

"I'll leave you to retire. Oh, and Laura and I are having coffee tomorrow evening. You need not join us."

He turned. And walked away.

Chapter 25

I kicked my bedroom door open so hard, my foot went through it, and I spent a few seconds hopping in the hallway, trying to pull my ankle free.

I finally staggered into the room, pulled off my Beverly Feldman flats, and threw them into the far wall. The leather might get scratched, but I didn't give a fuck.

That's right. *"I don't give a fuck!"* I screamed. "It's not fair! It's not fair! I did the right thing, I sent Nick away! I could totally have boned him silly, but I took the damned high road and for *what*? To have that jerk make me feel *worse*? To be *more* lonesome?"

I was hurling clothes away like a madwoman, searching

for my pajamas at the same time, and generally staggering around my room like a drunk.

I scooped up the Feldmans from their separate corners and went to put them away in their little cubby but ended up collapsing facedown on my closet floor, sobbing. I clutched the shoes to my (naked) chest and curled up (naked). I was probably getting tears on my Manolos, and I just didn't care.

"Betsy?"

I ignored it and cried harder. I was in no mood for the latest hell. Tina, telling me George had crocheted a ladder and was on the lam again? The Ant, telling me it was twins? The plant lady, telling me the plants were as dead as I was?

"Sweetie, why are you naked and crying in your closet?"

I cracked open an eye. Jessica was peering into the closet, a look of concern on her (bruised) face. "Go away," I cried. "Go away, you still hate me, I know it."

"Oh, shut up, I do not." She came into the closet, pushed suits aside, carefully moved shoes, and sat cross-legged beside me. "Come on, what's the matter?"

"Everything!"

"Right, but be specific."

"Sinclair doesn't love me anymore. I bet he doesn't even want to be the king anymore. I bet he's sorry he tricked me into the whole gig. And he's got the hots for my sister. My *sister!* Who's the daughter of the devil, but that's not even the worst part."

"What's the worst part, honey?"

"Everybody likes Laura, that's what."

"Everybody likes you, too. Even before you died you had this kind of cool charisma going."

"Yeah, but Laura has it in spades. She makes me look like Saddam Hussein. I mean, nobody can resist her."

"I'm sure that's not—"

"The *Ant* likes Laura!"

"Oh."

"And she and my dad are still wrecking my life—it was the longest baby shower ever. And I'm gonna have to file Chapter Eleven on Scratch. And she's—Laura, I mean— she's nice but she's no you. And then I could have had sex with Nick and he really likes me, but I love Sinclair so I sent him away, and Sinclair didn't even care and—and— oh my God!"

"Uh . . ." Jessica was obviously trying to puzzle out the babble.

"Oh my God! *I love Sinclair!* I love him! *Him!* That— that arrogant sneaky gorgeous cool sneaky—"

"Well, of course you do."

"See, this is the sort of information I could have used earlier," I said and cried harder.

Jessica was patting my back. "Come on, Bets, you knew

deep down you loved him. Like anyone could move into your house if you really didn't want them. Like you'd put up with all that from just any guy. Like you'd *sleep* with just any guy."

"But he's such a jerk."

"Well, sweetie, you're not the easiest person in the world to get along with, either, sometimes." She grinned and touched her black eye. "And this isn't even for losing your *Simpsons Season Four* DVD."

"Jess—I'm so sorry—I feel so bad—" I gestured to my nudity, the closet, the cedar balls.

"I know, Betsy." She bent down and kissed me, right on the temple. "I just had to sulk and, you know, heal up the last couple of days. I know you were sorry right after."

"I was, I was! I felt like dead dog shit. It's been the absolute worst week."

"Frankly, the only reason I've decided to forgive you is because I'm dying to meet the daughter of the devil."

"Oh, God, she's so boring." I sat up and wiped my dry (I didn't cry like a normal person anymore) eyes. "I mean, really nice. Don't get me wrong, she's a total sweetheart. You'll like her. But—"

"But she's no queen of the vampires."

"I haven't been much of a queen these days."

"That's not true. You read the Book so you could find

out more about yourself, about the threat to the world— your sister. And you tracked her down and were ready to rumble, until she turned out to be nice. And you're helping George."

"You *have* been listening to the baby monitor!"

"Are you kidding? That sucker's been on twenty-four hours a day. I was afraid to sleep; I didn't want to miss anything."

"Everything's such a mess."

"Worse than usual," she agreed.

"What am I going to do?"

"Well, honey, sending Nick away was a good start. It's actually fundamental, when you get right down to it."

"Oh, I know," I said earnestly. She could have suggested I boink the Green Bay Packers and I would have agreed. I was so happy she was talking to me again. "Er . . . when you say fundamental . . ."

She rolled her eyes, but then she was used to explaining things to me. "You sent Nick away because you didn't want to hurt him or take advantage of him. That's the kind of person you are—the kind you've always been. A lot has changed, but not that."

"You're right."

"Also, the sky is yellow, the Ant is misunderstood, and David Evins was just a talented amateur."

"Now you're just being mean."

"Well, I gotta milk this for all I can. And Sinclair doesn't love your sister."

"Not yet," I said darkly. "Give him time."

"Look, I'm sure he's interested in her—"

"Wait till you see her. Just wait."

"Like he doesn't have pussy thrown at him from cars?"

"What a horrifying mental image."

"I'm just saying, the guy can get laid whenever he wants. But he wants you."

"No, he—"

"Whatever you did to him after reading the Book," she said, and I don't think she was aware that she was touching her bruised eye while she reasoned stuff out, "can't undo how he feels. I'm telling you—I've *been* telling you—the guy is totally gonzo nuts for you, has been since the beginning. He's giving you the chilly treatment because his feelings are hurt. If he really didn't care about you, don't you think he'd just have shut up and fucked you?"

"I did think that," I admitted. "But he wasn't happy I had sex with him; he was hurt. I couldn't get why he was acting so weird, and it's too late now. He's been hearing me diss him for so long, he's given up."

"For so long? You've been a vampire for six months, Bets. That's nothing to him, it's a baseball season. Like I said, he's interested in your sister, sure. She's the daughter of the devil! And he's the king of the vampires. So of course he's gonna want to, you know, look into it. But I bet he's just covering his bases—being Sinclair."

"A real match made in heaven. Sinclair the star fucker and the woman fated to take over the world."

"She *would* be a pretty good consort for him," Jessica admitted.

"Anybody but me, that's for sure."

"Now, come on. The Book hasn't been wrong about anything yet—"

"The Book just said we'd be consorts, it didn't promise a happily ever after. Plenty of kings and queens ran things while hating each other." I'd minored in European history; Diana and Charles's marriage foundering before her death was nothing, historically speaking. "If you'd just heard how mean he's been—no, that's not right, not mean exactly, more like he doesn't give much of a shit."

"I did hear. I was starting to tell you, I'd been coming down to leave a check for Cathie—"

"The upstairs lady?"

"No, the plant lady."

"Jess, you don't have to pay someone just to water the plants. Five people live in this house, for Christ's sake. I'm sure we can handle it without—"

"*Anyway,* I sort of overheard your little *tête à lame* with Nick. And then I sort of overheard you and Sinclair. He was pretty frigid," she added, giving me a sympathetic look. "I'm sure it's not a total loss. But you've got some work to do."

I was trying not to be devastated by the blast of common sense she was giving my system. "Look, it's all on me, okay? I get that. I couldn't think of how to make it right with him. And to be honest, I thought I had bigger problems. So I just sort of put it out of my head, and then it was too late." I shook my head. "I've always assumed he'd be around to be, you know, yelled at and taken for granted. And of course I was wrong. Nobody's going to put up with that forever."

"Well, look. Put Sinclair aside for the moment. Actually, don't even do that—he's all wrapped up in this. Betsy, you can fix this."

"I don't think it's as easy as you—"

"I didn't say easy, I said fixable. And even if you couldn't fix it, you're not going to be all naked and weepy and whiney in your closet. I mean, come on. Crying in the closet? Honey, you're the *queen* of the *vampires*. Get your big white butt up off the floor and get dressed and start kicking some undead ass. Even before you died, you wouldn't take this shit lying down. So go fix it."

"You're right! Except for that thing about my butt." I was on my feet, my hands balled into fists. Mighty (and naked) would be my wrath! Jessica was right, who did they think they were fucking with? "You're totally right. I've been bending over, and for what? Well, forget about it!"

"Right!"

"I'm gonna right some wrongs, I'll tell you that right now!"

"Right! That's the girl."

I checked my watch, currently the only thing I was wearing (unless eyeliner counted). "And I'll tell you what we're doing first."

"Besides putting on underpants?"

"Right, besides that."

Chapter 26

"You're really gonna do it?"

"Bet your ass."

"It didn't really cause any of your problems."

"No," I agreed, "but it's dangerous. It's just lying around in the library for anybody to pick up and read."

"It's irreplaceable."

"So was the Nazi regime. Besides, I promised my mom I wouldn't burn it." We were standing on one of the big bridges connecting the suburbs with Minneapolis, and talking loudly to be heard over the hum of traffic. It was chilly—maybe forty degrees—but I was so hyped up I barely noticed. "So it's gonna sleep with the fishes."

I shoved, and the Book of the Dead went down and

down (it was a high bridge), and then plopped into the Big Muddy.

"Huh," Jessica said after a long moment of watching it sink out of sight with nary a bubble. "I guess I thought it would float on a bed of pure evil, or whatever."

"It's made out of skin, not Gore-Tex." I brushed off my chilly hands. "Boy, was that a relief or what? I should have done that months ago."

"Yep, that's that." Jessica zipped her coat higher. "Now what?"

"I don't know, but it's gonna be something, you know, take-chargish."

"Oh, good."

"And stay out of the basement."

"I don't think George would hurt me. Not on a full stomach, anyway."

"All the same."

"Don't worry. One vampire attack a week is my limit."

I hadn't had much time to effect change in my life—I'd talked with Jessica for hours, then destroyed a priceless artifact, and that had pretty much burned up my night. But after sleeping through the next day, I rose around six ready to kick some passive-aggressive vampire ass. First stop: Scratch.

On the way out to my car, I thought about trying to find Eric and doing something embarrassing like telling him I loved him, but chickened out. Also, I wasn't sure it would change anything. The last thing I could stand was being a burden—on anyone. If he didn't feel the same way—or worse, if he once had but didn't anymore—I wasn't going to be all Scarlett O'Hara ("Where will I go? What shall I do?") on him.

But at least I knew, now. It was sort of a relief to have it at the top of my mind, instead of lurking deep in my subconscious. But realizing—okay, admitting—I loved Eric Sinclair didn't solve anything. Real life was messy, and loving him didn't magically undo the old problems and make everything wonderful and perfect. In fact, it sort of made a few things worse.

If you took anything wrong in my life—"I'm upset Eric tricked me and made himself king" or "I'm upset Eric didn't tell me about my sister and Satan"—and tacked on "and I love Eric Sinclair," it made things messier.

Irony: loving Eric Sinclair and having it be another on a long list of problems. But now was the time for action! I was all done crying naked in the closet, thank you very much. I would be the mistress—queen, if you will—of my own destiny!

Starting with Scratch. I knew that place could make money; the vampires were sulking and not helping me.

I needed to put a little fear of the queen into the undead. And I needed to have Margarita Mondays.

I drove around for what seemed like half an hour, looking for a parking ramp that wasn't full, then finally gave up and parked in one of the handicap spaces just down the block. I felt a twinge of conscience but managed to squash it; being dead had to count as some sort of handicap. For the millionth time, I reminded myself to get a Manager Parking spot put out front.

I stormed through the door and stood in the nearly empty (groan . . . on a Friday night!) bar. "All right, listen up!" I began, only to be cut off by Klaus.

"Oh good, you've decided to drop by," he snarked.

"Hey, hey. I've had other things going on."

"Other things besides being the queen."

"Well, yeah. I mean no! It's all sort of wrapped up in . . ." I trailed off. Why was I explaining myself to this yutz? This was not part of the Take Charge plan. "Listen, things are going to be different from here on out."

"You're right about that," a vampire I didn't know piped up from her seat at the bar.

"Who's talking to *you*?"

"The employees of Scratch are now officially on strike," Klaus announced. He looked at his watch. "As of 6:59 p.m."

"You're *what*?"

"On strike."

I was having trouble processing this. "You're *what*?"

"We have formed a union," he continued, "to demand proper working conditions."

"And proper working conditions would be . . . ?" I had a horrible suspicion what they were.

"We want sheep to be allowed here, we want to be able to drink blood on the dance floor—"

"And at the bar," another vampire said. He was a pale brunette in a denim jacket, sitting next to the woman who'd spoken up earlier.

"Right, at the bar . . ." Slight Overbite was ticking the demands off on his long, spidery (yerrrrgggh) fingers. "And if a sheep becomes difficult, or a human wanders in, we want to be able to have a little fun."

"Kill them," I clarified.

"Right. Also, we want a dental plan."

"Really?" I gasped.

"No." He grinned, a wholly unpleasant image. "That last one was a joke."

"This whole *thing* is a joke. You guys are seriously nuts if you think I'm going to allow *any* of that. In case you didn't get the memo, we are, as of Nostro biting the big one, a friendlier vampire nation."

"You'd pull our fangs," he spat.

"I'd have you act decently!" We were nose to upturned

nose. "What *is* it with you guys? You're dead, so you have to be assholes?"

"We don't have to be," the woman at the bar admitted. "We just like to. You can't change hundreds of years of mystic evolution."

"Sure I can. That 'we're going to do it because we can' crap doesn't fly with me. Now: as for being on strike, you're not on strike, you're fired. I can get anybody to run this place. You don't like the working conditions? Fuck off and die. Again."

"This is your last chance to change your mind," Denim Boy said. Like I was scared of anybody wearing a Tommy Hilfiger knockoff.

"No," I said. "It's yours."

"You're not leaving us with a lot of breathing room," a new voice said. For a place I'd thought was practically deserted, there were a shitload of vampires suddenly around.

"Fortunately," Klaus said, "we don't need any."

Another vampire came out from the back, dragging— uh-oh—Laura. He had a bunch of her perfect blond hair in his fist, right by her skull, and she had both hands on his and was stumbling, trying not to trip.

"Surprise," she said, trying to smile.

Chapter 27

"Cheaters!" I cried.

"We were so happy to make your sister's acquaintance."

"I'll bet, ya big cheater."

"Eric canceled our meeting," she said, "and I had a free evening, so I thought I'd come and see you."

"Well, next time, call first."

"I got that," she said.

"It was almost too good to be true," Asshole said. "It's so rare to find a vampire with any living relatives. And to have one walk into our hands . . ."

"Right! Rare. Don't you guys think that's weird? I mean, look how young she is. She's not my great-great-granddaughter, she's my kid sister. Doesn't that tell you something about me? Like maybe you shouldn't be messing with me?"

"I figure they don't like their working conditions," Laura said helpfully, still clutching the vampire's hand. "But this seems kind of extreme."

"Maybe your *mother* could help us out," I said, then waited. We all waited. Laura looked puzzled—or maybe she was rolling her eyes, I couldn't tell. "You know, your *mother* could show up and, you know, give us a hand."

Nothing. Humph! Typical. The devil: never around when you needed her.

"Look, you don't want to do this," I told Klaus and the cow at the bar and Tommy Hilfiger. "You really don't."

"I think she's right," Laura said, practically up on her toes. "I think you should try a walkout first. I think hostage-taking should be a second resort. Maybe third."

The vampire jerked her head, and she cried out.

I rubbed my eyes. I had to admit, I hadn't foreseen this.

What should I do? What if I lied and told them they could have their sheep and their homicide and their kill-one-get-one-free Thursdays, got Laura out of danger, then reneged? Could a queen go back on her word? The other vampires might lose respect for me . . . well, more respect.

"Before we get into this any further, I just want to clarify: What exactly do you guys think happened to Nostro and Monique?"

"The king helped you."

"Okay. And, just for the record, do you see the king around anywhere right now?"

Klaus hesitated. "No."

"I better leave one of you alive, then. I'm getting really tired of this 'Sinclair must have helped her' bullshit. If one of you spreads the word about me, that would really help me out."

"Ouch! That *really* hurts," Laura said to the vampire fisting her hair. "Will you please let go?"

"Shut up, sheep."

"Are you particularly attached to this man?" Laura asked me.

"I've never even *met* him."

"Oh, okay. I really, really hope this doesn't give you the wrong impression."

"Wh—" was as far as I got before a shaft of reddish gold light burst from the vampire's stomach, and he evaporated. Or vaporized. Or something—he didn't even have time to scream, it was that fast.

I screamed. Not very monarchlike, it's true. But I couldn't help it. See, in real life, vampires didn't disappear when they were killed. They didn't collapse into a dramatic dust pile or burst into flames, short of direct exposure to sunlight. They didn't even die when you poked them in the gut.

You stuck a stake in their chests and/or cut their heads off, and they died forever. They didn't get back up. Well, I did that one time, but that was a special case.

But other than sunlight cases, there was always a body, no matter what you did.

Laura was standing by herself, patting her hair down with her right hand and holding a—I guess it was sword of sorts—in her left. Proof! Proof she was hell spawned . . . she was a lefty!

"Sorry about that," she said. "But I just couldn't stand to have his hands on me another second. Yuck."

"What is *that*?" I gasped.

She glanced at the flame-colored sword. It glowed with such heat, it was actually a little hard to look at. "Oh, this?" she asked, like I was asking her about a new bracelet. "Well. I can forge weapons from hellfire."

"And you can *kill* people with that?"

"Not people," she said helpfully. "I'll be glad to fill you in later."

"This—ah—this changes—changes nothing," Klaus said, looking like he was trying not to barf. I knew the feeling. "We still—we still—ah—demand—demand—"

"You have to get close with that," Tommy Hilfiger said. "You can't get us all in arrgghh!" He said "arrgghh" because, quick as thought, Laura's sword changed to a crossbow, and she shot Tommy from across the room. He vanished in a puff of light, just like the other one.

She lowered the crossbow to her side and looked modest. Which she actually pulled off. She was so beautiful, she looked like a fairy-tale princess. With a weapon of mass vampire destruction.

"Ha-*ha*!" I crowed. "How about that, Klaus the mouse? Hah? Hah?"

"Wait a minute." I turned to Laura. "You know we're all vampires?"

"Sure."

"And you were going to tell me when?"

"I was waiting for you to tell *me*," she said, having the nerve to sound offended.

"But how did you *know*?"

"Sometimes I just . . . figure things out. I guess I get that from my mother." She looked disgusted, like having anything in common with her mother was a revolting thought.

"Your mother."

More disgust. "The devil."

"You know. Your mom. Is the devil."

"Her mom is the devil?" the lady at the bar asked in a hushed voice.

"And you let me take you to the Ant's baby shower and

never said anything? And brought her a present? And had *two* slices of carrot cake? And *talked* to her?" I was trying to figure out which was more annoying: yet another vampire coup or Laura keeping her mouth shut all this time.

"Well, *you* never told me you were the queen of the vampires," she said hotly.

"That's totally a different thing!" I cried.

"I wanted to get a chance to meet the woman who carried me for nine months."

"And then *dumped* you at a hospital."

"Yes, but when you compare that to, you know, being Satan, it doesn't seem so bad. In fact, it's downright friendly."

She had me on that one. "Laura, don't you get what this means? Your *mom* is *Satan*!"

"Of course I get what it means. Besides, I don't think your parents define who you are," she reasoned.

I opened my mouth to yell some more, only to get cut off. "Excuse me," Klaus said, sounding peeved, "but you have other business to attend to right now."

"It's not more interesting than this, pal," I said. "Vampires being sneaky and up to no good is so *not* anything new."

"She's too dangerous," the woman at the bar said, "to live another five minutes."

"Which one of us is she talking about?"

"Does it matter?" Laura asked.

Klaus said something in rapid French—I think it was French. The door to the back room opened, as did the front door, and all kinds of waitresses and bartenders and bouncers started streaming in. They were all pale and twitchy and pissed-off.

"As far as plans go, it's not the worst one I've ever seen," Laura said. "But you'll die if you all try to jump us at once."

"You got what he said?"

"Oh, I'm really good at languages."

"Which ones?" I asked, curious.

"All of them."

Of course. "Look, she's right. Can't we sit down and discuss this like civilized dead people and hell spawn?"

"Please don't call me that."

"I'm sorry! Just please don't shoot me or stab me."

Laura looked mildly crushed. "I wouldn't do that, Betsy."

"Sorry again."

"You can't—" Klaus said, and then lunged at me. Aha! The old 'keep a placid look on your face and talk normally and then jump them' trick. Unfortunately, it totally worked; he bowled right into me, and we went sprawling backward, knocking a table aside. Several vampires, I was sorry to see, leapt onto us to help.

"Nothing—is—more—important—than—this!" Klaus shouted, punctuating each word by smacking my head onto the floor. It was fairly easy for him because he had both hands around my throat. The guy was quick *and* strong; he had a grip like an angry anaconda.

"Au contraire," I gurgled, and then I couldn't say anything at all. What was he doing, strangling a dead girl? That couldn't really hurt me; it was mostly just annoying. *Must be plenty pissed,* I thought.

I was digging my fingers into his hands to pry them off, but his grip never loosened, and the flesh was just peeling away in strips. Blurgh! Death loomed (again), *and* I was grossed out. It was the worst week ever. Again.

Chapter 28

"Not like this!" a vampire I didn't know was shouting into Klaus's ear. "We can't attack the queen! We all agreed not to attack the queen!"

Yeah, I wanted to shout, but couldn't say a word. I just made an agreeable sort of peep while I clawed at his hands some more.

"She's not the queen," he muttered and jerked one of his elbows back, straight into Sane and Helpful Vampire's throat. It didn't appear to hurt the guy, but it knocked him back. Even better, it caused Klaus's grip to loosen. I managed to get my hands up between his and shoved and kicked at the same time. He didn't get off me, but his grip fell away.

"It's times like this when I like to say a prayer," I said, still kicking and clawing for all I was worth, trying to get out from under him. It was the Homecoming Dance all over again! "The Lord is my Shepherd, I shall not want. Also, God is great, God is good, let us thank him for this food. Also, Jesus loves me this I know, for the Bible tells me so." Since Klaus was now screaming and clutching his ears, when I kicked him again, he finally flew off me. I rose up on my elbows and finished triumphantly, "And *God bless this mess!*"

I was fresh out of Bible verses, but the damage had been done. Sane and Helpful Vampire had already flung the door open and was frantically gesturing for the others to follow him. Some did—I'd worry about them later—but a distressing number stayed. Including Klaus, who had backed all the way up to the bar, his face twisted with hate and fear, his hands still clamped over his ears.

Laura was coughing a little and waving her hand in front of her face, and I saw that the half dozen or so vampires that had been around her were now—gone. Vaporized. All but the last one. Laura's crossbow was a sword again, and she blocked a fist with her forearm, then stuck the woman (formerly "the woman at the bar") right in the chest. Bye-bye, annoying barfly.

"Ha-*ha!*" I crowed, pointing. "How about that? Hah? *Hah?* Didn't figure on her being hell sp—I mean, the devil's daughter when you grabbed her, didja?" Another vampire had me by the hair and was yanking me backward, but I didn't care. *"Didja?"* I was practically delirious with triumph.

"Betsy—" was as far as my wonderful, supertalented, too-cool sister got before she had her hands full again. I noticed that in addition to the kickass hellfire weapons, she was a pretty fair hand-to-hand fighter. Sometime in the last few years while she was finishing Bible school and volunteering for church bake sales, she'd picked up a black belt or two along the way. Now if I could just get her to wear some decent clothes . . .

"Don't worry about me," I called, though my skull was throbbing like a rotten tooth. "Everything's under contr—yeeouch!"

"Shut up, bitch," someone growled.

"Oh, *you* shut up," I snapped back. "Do you have any idea how often this happens to me? It's almost boring." And terrifying. But mostly boring.

Two more—not that there were that many left, thanks to Laura and their cowardice—came straight at me, and I heard the ominous sound of a chair leg being snapped off. The other one had me in a firm grip, his arm across my throat, his other hand still in my hair. Holding me nice and still. Well, the joke was on him! Stakes in the chest didn't work on me, so there. Of course, it was going to hurt like hell, and ruin my shirt, and if they decided to give 110 percent and cut my head off after, that could pose difficulties. I could buy a new shirt, but I kind of needed the head I had.

I opened my mouth to torture them with more psalms, when Laura got to the one on the right—stab, poof! It was amazing. I could never describe how cool it was, not in a thousand pages. She looked like an avenging angel with her shiny hair and demure bangs, her nondescript clothing, and the sword that actually hurt to look at, held so comfortably in her fist.

The vampire on the left was suddenly yanked out of sight, and there was a sickening crunch as he hit the wall. Courtesy of—I nearly gasped—Eric Sinclair. He'd come out of nowhere—probably pushing his way past the stream of frantically exiting vampires—and just grabbed the nearest one and shoved. The vampire bounced off the wall and hit the floor, and I could see where his entire face had actually been pushed in by the force of smacking into the concrete. The worst part of it was, it hadn't killed him. He moved feebly on the floor like a stunned beetle, trying to grow his nose back.

"Oh, guh-*ross*!" I screamed.

"Wow," Laura goggled.

"Take your hands off her," Sinclair told the guy behind me, "or they'll write books about what I'll do to you."

The vampire let go of me so quick, he yanked out a handful of my hair. I yelped and shook free of him.

Suddenly, surprisingly, it was just the three of us in Scratch—two vampires had picked up the guy who needed a new face, and they scrammed.

Oh, wait—four. Klaus was in the corner, showing his teeth like one of those little ratty dogs that liked to challenge everyone from the mailman to the preschooler.

Sinclair turned to him, but I held up a hand. "Tut, tut, my good man. I'll take care of this. Strike on *me,* will you? Form a union in *my* club, willya?"

"For shame," Laura added.

"Shut up, devil's whore," Klaus spat.

"Don't you call her that!" I said, shocked. "She's the farthest thing from a whore in the whole world. You're just mad because death is imminent."

He snarled at me. It would have been scarier if Eric hadn't been right at my elbow. "This isn't over yet, *Betsy.*"

"Excellent," I said. "I would also have accepted 'You haven't seen the last of me' and 'You'll regret this.'" Then I picked up the discarded chair leg and ran it into his chest. (You'd think, since it was a vampire bar, they'd have metal chairs.) Sayonara, Slight Overbite.

Unlike Laura's more dramatic death-dealing, he just toppled over, which forced the stake farther into his body (ugh), and lay there like a big old dead bug.

Now that *that* was over with, I had several impulses. I picked one and rushed to Laura and hugged her. "Wow, Laura, you were amazing! I'm so sorry I got you into such a mess, but wow! How cool were you?"

"I hope you don't think I'm a bad person," she explained. "Violence isn't usually the answer. But they didn't seem amenable to listening to reason, and I didn't want you to get hurt."

"You didn't want *me* to get hurt? Laura, you're amazing! How did you do that? How come it's a sword sometimes and a bow some other times? Can it do anything else? Did your mother give it to you?"

She laughed and twirled the sword in a small circle so the hilt was in her palm and not her fist, then sheathed it at her right hip—except she wasn't wearing a sheath. The sword just disappeared. Except I had the distinct impression it was still there.

Waiting.

I turned to Sinclair. "And you! Not that I'm not glad to see you, but—"

"Elizabeth!" I eeped and nearly cowered away from him; I'd never seen him so furious. His dark eyes were slits, and even his hair looked angry—it was messy and I squished the urge to straighten it with my fingers. His white shirt was open at the throat, and he was sockless and coatless. He'd come in a hurry. "What were you thinking, instigating a brawl with two dozen vampires?"

"I didn't start it," I said, shocked. He was holding my shoulders, and his fingers were actually biting into me. "I told them they couldn't kill people, and then they went on strike! Which isn't as nonviolent as it sounds, by the way."

"You might have been killed," he said through gritted teeth. "You must never, *never* do such a thing again."

"But *I* didn't do anythinmmmmmph!" He'd yanked me to him and planted one on me, effectively cutting off my protest. I was so surprised he was kissing me—surprised he was mad at all—I just stood there for a moment and took it. Then I managed to pull away—or at least pull my lips away. My head was arched back like a snake's, but our chests were touching.

"Wait, wait, wait. I'm really glad to see you. But I'm confused."

He quirked a small smile at me. "Thus, the universe resumes its axis."

"Never mind about the universe." I gave in to my impulse, managed to free an arm, and straightened his hair. "I thought you were making moves on Laura."

"I've been meeting with her," he replied, looking confused.

"Right, but I thought—you know, after what happened, after I made you have sex with me—"

"Twice," he added. I could tell he was trying not to laugh. "After you raped me twice. Well, one and a half times."

"Um, yeah. I thought you didn't like me anymore."

He looked astonished. "Didn't *like* you?"

"And then Laura—she's so beautiful and her breasts are so perky."

"Thank you," Laura called from behind the bar, where she was fixing herself a Shirley Temple.

"And you were so mean to me—"

"I was a little cold," he admitted, his grip loosening. He didn't let go entirely, I noticed.

"A little?"

"It hurt me that you only made love with me because you had gone insane."

"I can't hear any of this," Laura announced, dropping a cherry into her drink. "Just carry on like I'm not here."

We did. "I'm sorry. But I wouldn't want you to think I only want to have sex with you when I'm crazy."

"I don't. I hung on to the notion that you were motivated by more than the impulse to hurt. And, truthfully, I could never leave you. Certainly not after you were vulnerable to the Book. I thought it was odd that the devil's own should show up—was so easily found—right after you read the Book. I dislike coincidences. So I resolved to find out as much about her as I could."

"So they were like—like business meetings?" I was starting to feel dumber than usual. He was looking at me so earnestly, and he still hadn't let go. Maybe because I hadn't asked him to. "You weren't interested in her as, like, a date?"

"I couldn't be with *him*," Laura said, so shocked she actually set down her drink with a clunk and a slosh. "He's a vampire!"

"And I couldn't be with her," he said, "because she isn't you. Oh, and for your information, dear," he added mildly, glancing over at her, "once you go undead, you never go back."

"Yuck! And Betsy. I can't believe you thought I'd try to steal your boyfriend," she said reproachfully.

"Consort," Sinclair corrected.

"I'm sorry. To both of you, I'm sorry. I guess I jumped to some pretty dumb conclusions." I hugged him. "I've never been so happy to be wrong! And with all the practice I have, you'd think—"

He pulled back and looked at me. "Elizabeth, even if I did not adore you, you are my queen. We're fated to be together. I've known that since the moment I saw you in the crypt."

"That's so romantic," Laura sighed, rinsing her glass.

"Sinclair—Eric—" Why did the most meaningful moments of my life happen in front of witnesses? "I—I adore you, too. Well, I don't know if I adore you. That's not really the word I'd use. But I—I—" I managed to wrench it out. God, this was hard! "I love you."

"Of course you do," he said, totally unsurprised.

"*What?* I finally tell you my deepest, most personal feelings and you're all, 'Yeah, I already got that memo'? This, *this* is why you drive me nuts! This is why it's hard to tell you things! I take it back."

"You can't take it back," he said smugly.

"I do, too, take it back! And don't you dare kiss me again!" I cried when he leaned forward. "Why do you have to be so annoying and smug all the time?"

"Because with you by my side, I can do anything."

I calmed down a little. He was still acting way too superior, but that was kind of sweet. In a frightening, world-domineering way. "Well . . . well, I guess I don't take it back. Not entirely."

"Of course you don't."

I almost snarled. "I guess I really do love you."

"And I you, darling Elizabeth. I cherish you, my own, my dear one."

Okay, now I was *really* calming down. "Well. Okay."

"Where are the darned napkins?" Laura sobbed from the bar.

He reached out and smoothed a lock of my hair behind my ear. "You're wearing my necklace."

I touched the small platinum shoe he had given me when he got back from Europe—had it only been a few days ago? "Well, yeah. I wanted it tonight . . . for luck, you know?"

He smiled. "Were you really jealous? You thought I was wooing Laura?"

"Maybe a little. You're not smirking, are you?"

"No, no." He smothered a snicker. "I am sorry for giving you cause for doubt."

"Oh, like you didn't notice she's fantastically beautiful," I bitched.

"She is not you," he replied simply, which was flattering, yet slippery of him.

"Eric . . . the thing about doubt . . ." I groped for the words. This was my chance. Maybe my only one. He was an all-powerful vampire king, but he wasn't a telepath. "I would feel more—together—with you, I mean—if we—if you and I—if we got married."

"But we are married," he said, puzzled.

"Not Book of the Dead married. *Really* married, with a minister—well, a judge—and my mom there and cake and hymns—songs—and a ring and dancing."

"Oh." He looked sort of horrified. "Well. Ah. I see."

"You see? Now? Why not before? It's one of the things I complain about constantly."

"Question asked, question answered."

I let that pass. "Look, I know this is probably getting old, but I was kind of shoved into this whole consort thing. I don't know a lot about you; we don't have this deep, meaningful relationship."

"To be fair, I think that's just as much your fault as his," Laura said, munching on olives. When we both looked at her, she said, "I'm sorry. But that's the impression I got."

"*Anyway.* A real-person wedding would—I would really love that."

"But we are already married." Sinclair seemed to be having trouble actually grasping my essential problem.

"But I don't feel it."

"And a real"—the corners of his mouth turned down, as if he was contemplating a fresh dog turd instead of getting married—"wedding . . . would help you feel it?"

"Totally."

Sinclair clasped my hands. "You are so immature," he said, looking deeply into my eyes, "that you take my breath away."

I jerked my hands out of his grip. "Aw, shaddup. And you don't even need to breathe. Yes or no, pal?"

He sighed. "Yes."

I was shocked. "Really? Yes? You'll do it?"

"Of course. You had only to ask."

"*I* had only to ask? See, this is part of the problem. You—"

"Elizabeth, darling. Shut up." Then he kissed me again.

Chapter 29

"You're getting *married?*" Marc's jaw was hanging down. We were sitting in the kitchen having hot chocolate and toast. Jessica was sitting on Marc's other side, and Tina and Sinclair were sitting on my right. I nearly sighed with the pleasure of it; things were finally getting back to normal. "A wedding? A vampire wedding?"

"You keep saying that; you sound like a crackpot parrot."

"Better be a midnight ceremony," he shot back.

"Yeah, I guess. That's okay. We could do like a roses in the garden midnight theme, with masses of red and white flowers everywhere . . ." Was that a shudder from Sinclair? He was studying the financial pages and didn't appear to be paying attention, but I knew damn well he was listening to every word. I narrowed my eyes and started to say something but was foiled by Tina.

"When is the date?"

"We haven't decided yet. I thought Easter, but that—uh, well, maybe next fall."

"Autumn's good," Jessica said. "We'll need time to plan." That *was* a shudder! Before I could act, she went on. "But you're still going to live here, right? There's plenty of room."

"Of course," Sinclair said absently, turning a page. "This is our headquarters. I see no reason to leave. Though," he added with a sly look, "you might forgo rent as a wedding gift."

"Forget it." Jessica eyed my shoe necklace and grinned. "Well, maybe for a month."

"Can we get back to the death and betrayal and all that?" Marc broke in. He was so intent, he dropped his toast into his tea. Oh, wait. That was the way he ate it. Shudder. "So the workers at Scratch turned on you? And you *and* Miss Goody-goody killed them?"

"Don't call her that. And yeah, most of them," I clarified. "Some of them got away while the getting was good."

"They're like rats that way." Jessica saw the look Tina was giving her and added defensively, "Come on. They jump her when they think they can get away with it, then get the hell gone when it goes bad. It's not the first time, that's for sure.

I *know* you're not getting all offended on behalf of all vampire kind."

"No," she admitted.

"Steps will be taken," Sinclair said, still not looking up from the paper. What an irritating habit. I'd have to work on that after the wedding.

"Indeed," Tina said. "With all respect, Majesty, I wish you would have said something when you left. You shouldn't have gone there alone. It's my place to take on danger."

"Which one of them are you talking to?" Marc asked.

I giggled but sobered up when Eric clarified. "There wasn't time," he said simply.

"How'd you even know to go there?" I asked. "I've been wondering about that for hours."

Jessica coughed. "I might have given him an earful."

"That's one way of putting it," he said, looking wry. "I didn't rush there to save you. I rushed there to—" He looked around at the group. We were all hanging on his every word. But then, he had that kind of effect on people. "That is a . . . private matter . . . between Elizabeth and me. Needless to say, I was annoyed to find the queen in trouble yet again."

"One more time, pal: Not. My. Fault."

"You always. Say. That."

"Well, maybe after the wedding the other vampires will

respect you more." Marc saw the frosty looks and added, "Well, they sure couldn't respect her *less*."

Since I'd had that exact thought earlier, I was hardly in a position to bitch. About that. Instead I said, "I think what's the most amazing thing—"

"Besides planning to supervise an appetizer menu for people who don't eat," Sinclair muttered.

"—is how remarkable Laura was. You guys. You wouldn't have believed it. She was slaughtering vampires left and right. It was the coolest!" When Sinclair and Tina traded a look, I clarified. "Bad vampires. It wouldn't have been as cool if she'd been killing nice, gentle orphan vampires."

"With a sword made of light?" Tina asked.

"Uh, hellfire, I think. If we're getting technical. And sometimes it's a crossbow. And it appears and disappears whenever she wants it."

"That makes sense," Marc said. I couldn't tell if he was joking.

"But she's so nice," Jessica said. "I haven't met her yet, but that's all you and Eric talk about, how nice she is."

"Yes," Tina said, "and that's interesting, isn't it? Is it an act, do you think?"

"No," Sinclair and I said in unison.

"Hmmm."

Sinclair put the paper down and picked up a pen and

scribbled more of that language in the margin. At least it wasn't a hate note. I was pretty sure. I'd never noticed he wrote everything down in Latin or whatever it was. "I suggest we get to know her better, and not just because she is family." He looked at me. "Will be family. After the wedding. The . . . wonderful, wonderful wedding."

"I'm having supper with Laura tomorrow," I said. "I figure I owe her a cocoa at the very least. I can ask her some stuff. But she seems kind of private."

Marc snorted. "I'll bet."

Chapter 30

$\mathcal{I}$ paused outside Sinclair's bedroom. The sun would be up soon, and just thinking about the night's events (not to mention living through them) made me tired. But now what? I'd told Sinclair the truth . . . told myself the truth. I knew he shared my feelings. We were engaged. We lived together. We were apparently in love. So did we share a bedroom? Did we wait until our wedding night?

My unholy lust for Sinclair's delicious bad self aside, I wanted to share a bed with him. I wanted to make up for using him earlier, and I wanted to hear his deep voice in the dark. And in my head.

On the other hand, after what I'd done to him earlier, what right did I have to expect us to literally kiss and make up? If our situations had been reversed, I'd have held a grudge for at least a year. Maybe I should give him time.

On the *other* other hand, he had come to Scratch specifically to . . . what? Regardless, he'd saved my ass yet again. Maybe it was silly to be all "you can have space, big guy."

Oh boy, was I pooped. Screw it. I'd worry about it tomorrow night.

I turned away and plodded down the hall to my room. One thing—well, another thing—to worry about; I had the master bedroom, which in a place like this was really saying something. After we got married, Sinclair would probably want to share it with me. That could be a problem; he was as picky about his suits as I was about my shoes. There was room in my heart for Sinclair, but was there room in my closet?

I opened my door and gaped. Sinclair was in my bed, shirtless (at least!), blankets up to his waist, poring over all kind of dusty books. He looked up. "Oh, there you are. Ready for bed?"

I clutched the knob. Uh, the doorknob. "Don't you think this is a little presumptuous?"

"No."

"I debated outside your door and decided to give you space!"

"How sweet. Please strip now."

I snorted, torn between irritation, arousal, and plain old

happiness. One thing about Eric Sinclair: he didn't dither. "Okay," I said, shutting the door. "But don't think it will be this easy every night."

"I'm counting on it, actually. Do you know, you're the only woman who has ever refused me?"

"No wonder you're such a pain."

"Tina had the same theory," he said thoughtfully. "But I dismissed it."

I pulled my T-shirt over my head, struggled out of my jeans, then stripped off my bra and panties. I shoved a few smelly books out of the way, ignoring his wince, and wriggled under the covers.

"Sushi socks?" he asked.

"What is it with you and Japanese cuisine? You don't like my sushi jammies, you don't like my socks . . ."

He smirked. "It's possible they're hurting the mood."

"Hey, it's chilly in here."

"If I warm you up," he said, pulling me against his chest, "will you take them off?"

"Done and done," I said, and opened my mouth against his. His hands circled my rib cage and then moved up, and it was all very fine. Whatever had happened between us, this moment seemed exactly right.

I reached down and felt him beneath my hand, already hard, and had a second to wonder—How *did* vampires get it up? Then I forgot about it as his hands cupped my bottom and pulled me closer, so close you couldn't have slipped a piece of Saran Wrap between us. He broke the kiss and pressed his lips to the hollow of my throat.

Oh Elizabeth, Elizabeth, at last, at last.

I nearly sighed with relief. I could hear him in my head again! I definitely wasn't evil anymore. Not that I had worried too much about it, but I *had* missed the intimacy of it.

"I love you," I said.

Elizabeth, oh my Elizabeth. His grip tightened, and after a long moment he murmured against my neck, "I love you, too. I've always loved you." *Always. Always.*

"You can bite me if you wa—" And then his teeth were in me, his tongue was pressed firmly against my throat, and we shuddered together. Only when Eric bit me did I feel like everything was wonderful. Only with Eric did I not mind being dead. In fact, being with Eric was the opposite of being dead.

"Oh, G—oh, thath good."

He stopped drinking so he could laugh, and I leaned down and tickled his balls. "Don't thtart or I'll thing a hymn."

"Anything but that, darling. You should practice more, get used to the scent."

"I only like doing that with you," I said, and he bit me again, on the other side.

And I you, you are sweet, you are like wine, you are . . . everything.

"Ummm . . ." I was shivering like I had a fever; God, I wanted him so much. "Come inside me now. I've waited long enough. Don't start about it being my own fault."

He laughed again and eased into me; I wrapped my legs around his waist and felt him slide all the way home. And oh, it was sweet, it was like wine, it was everything. I licked his throat and bit him, yes, it was like wine.

"Elizabeth," he groaned, thrusting hard. He grabbed my thighs, spread them apart for him, clamped down. Shoved, pushed, penetrated. And oh, it was good, it was so good. *Elizabeth, I love you, there's no one. No one.*

"Oh, boy," I gasped. That was it. That did it. I had thought my orgasm was way off, but it was just around the corner and when he said my name, when he *thought* my name, I could feel myself opening beneath his hands, his cock, his mouth, opening and coming, and it was more than fine, it was like coming home.

"Listen," he said, and his voice—it was trembling. I was shocked, even in the depths of my pleasure . . . I'd never heard him sound like that before. "Elizabeth. Listen to me. Don't do that again. Run off like that. Scare me again. Do you promise?"

Well, I didn't exactly run off, I was just trying to take

charge of things, and I certainly didn't set out to scare him, but—

"*Do you promise?*"

"Yes, yes, I promise. I didn't mean to scare you."

You are the only one who can scare me. "All right," he said, and his voice sounded normal again, thank goodness. He reached down and gently thumbed my clit, and this time when I shuddered, he did, too.

It took a long time for me to move, and I just sort of wriggled out from beneath him and flopped over like a fish. He groaned when I punched his shoulder to get him to give me a little room.

"Well, that was . . ." Orgasmic? Too obvious. Earthshaking? Too clichéd. Fantastically amazingly wonderful? Too needy.

He picked up my hand and kissed the knuckles. "Sublime."

"Ah! *Luh mot just.*"

He laughed. "Close enough."

I hesitated. It was obvious to me, and had been from the beginning, that he didn't know I could pick up his thoughts when we were having sex (when I wasn't evil). And I had never been able to figure out a way to tell him. He was so controlled, so cool and calm, I didn't know how to say it without freaking him out or making him mad. Hell, I could hardly explain it to myself; I'd *never* been able to read minds before, and I couldn't read anyone else's.

But now was the time. Things had never been better between us, more comfortable, more natural. In fact, I had never been happier, felt more loved, so safe. I would tell him, and he wouldn't freak out, and everything would still be nice between us.

"Good night, sweetheart," he said, and the sun slipped up in the sky—I couldn't see it, but I could feel it. I spun down and down into sleep.

And the moment passed.

Chapter 31

"So." I cleared my throat. "How 'bout those demonic powers?"

Laura wolfed down the last of her blueberry muffin. We were at the Caribou Coffee in Apple Valley, snarfing down muffins (well, she was) and white tea. After last night, I'd been tempted to cancel on her and spend the night in bed with Eric, but how many half sisters did I have? One, so far.

"Betsy, do you have something on your mind?"

"No, no. Well, maybe."

Laura's big blue eyes shone with reproach, which would have made me feel worse if there hadn't been crumbs sticking to her lower lip. "Everybody has secrets, Betsy. You most of all."

I handed her a napkin. "Hey, I'm totally open about my disgusting covert vampire lifestyle."

She laughed.

"Look, I just met you a few days ago, right? Heck, I just *found out* about you a few days ago. I couldn't think of a way to blurt out the whole 'I'm dead' thing without weirding you out. Or making you think I skipped my meds."

"You'd be surprised what does and doesn't weird me out."

"Hey, I was there, okay? I would totally not be surprised. Well, not that surprised. Look, let's do a *quid po ko*, okay?"

"I think," she said gently, "you mean *quid pro quo*."

"Right, right. Let's do one of those. I'll tell you something weirdly secret about me, and then you do the same."

"Um . . ."

"Oh, come on," I coaxed. "We're sisters, we have to get to know each other."

She fiddled with her glass. "Okay. You go first."

"Okay. Um . . . last night wasn't the first time a bunch of moody vampires tried to kill me."

She nodded. "Thank you for sharing that with me."

"Now it's your turn."

"Ah . . . when I was eight I stole a plastic whistle from Target."

"Laura!"

She cringed. "I know, I know. I felt so bad about it afterward I told my mom and my minister. Who was also my dad."

"For heaven's sake, what kind of morbid confession is that? I'm talking about really awful sinful evil stuff."

"Stealing *is* a sin."

I rested my forehead on the table. "I mean really bad stuff. Not kid stuff. Because I have something to tell you, and I can't do it if I don't feel a little closer to you."

Her eyes went round with curiosity. "Why can't you?"

Because I sucked at telling people intimate things about themselves. "Because I . . . I just have to."

"Well, why don't you just go ahead?" She patted the top of my head. "Just get it off your chest. You'll feel better."

"Okay. Well. You know how your mom is the devil and all . . . ?" Her lips thinned, but I plunged ahead. "And you know how—wait a minute. *How* do you know your mom is the devil?"

"My parents told me."

"Your mom and the minister?" I was trying not to gape at her, and failing.

"Yes."

"How did *they* know?"

"She told them. I think she thought it would be funny. That they would get rid of me. And she . . . the devil . . . appeared to me when I was thirteen." I noticed she didn't say "my mother." In fact, her lips were pressed together so

tightly, they had almost disappeared. "She told me everything. About possessing a—no offense, a woman of poor
character—"

"None taken. At all."

"—and how it was my destiny to take over the world
and how she was proud of me because I wasn't like anyone
else—"

The milk glass broke in her hands. It had been mostly
empty, but a little bit spilled onto the table, and I frantically blotted. Meanwhile, Laura was getting pretty
worked up.

"And it's not up to her, you know? It's not up to her at
all! It's my life, and I don't give a—a *crap* about destiny or
any of it. It doesn't mean anything anyway! I don't have to
be bad, and it's not how I was raised. *She* didn't raise me,
my mother and father did, and *she* doesn't get to decide
how I live my life, and that's how it is, that's how it is, that
is *exactly how it is*!"

This would have sounded like a normal antiparent rant
from any teenager, except while she was shouting, Laura's
honey blond hair shaded to a deep, true red and her big
blue eyes went poison green. I was leaning away from her
as far as I could get without actually falling on the floor,
and she was screaming into my face.

"Okay," I said. I would have held up my hands to placate
her, but if I let go, I'd be on my ass on the floor in Caribou

Coffee. "Okay, Laura. It's okay. Nobody's making you do anything."

She calmed a little. "I'm sorry. I just—she makes me crazy. So crazy."

"It's okay."

"I'm not like that."

"Okay."

"I won't be like that."

"Okay, Laura." I watched in fascination as her hair lightened and lightened until it was back to blond, as her eyes went from squinty and green to big and blue.

"It's like I said before. I don't think your parents define who you are."

"Definitely not." I was trying to look around the coffee shop without her seeing. How had nobody noticed her transformation? "I didn't mean to get you upset."

"It's not your fault." She was nervously picking up the pieces of the glass and piling them into a napkin. "I'm—I guess I'm a little sensitive on that subject."

Well, I won't be broaching that *one again, Red, not to worry.*

"So, uh, thanks again for your help last night." I tugged on a hank of her (blond?) hair. "I couldn't have done it without you."

She didn't smile back. "Yes, I know."

Chapter 32

"I have *got* to meet this woman!" Jessica gasped.

"It was unreal," I announced. "Totally, massively unreal. Honestly, I was afraid to take my eyes off her. And then she got over it and she was as nice as chocolate pie again."

"Huh. Did scary magical stuff happen?"

"Nothing besides the evil hair and colored contacts. Oh, and she gorged herself on four more muffins."

"That *is* evil."

"I know! She's as thin as a stick."

Jessica handed George a navy blue skein of yarn. We were in the basement, where she had fixed up his little concrete room with curtains (duct-taped to the walls), a mattress, lots of blankets, and about sixty pillows. An entire corner of the room had been taken up with a rainbow of crochet chains. George only knew one stitch. Still, the fact that he was stitching and not stabbing was a relief.

He didn't seem to mind Jessica poking around in his room, though we were careful—she was never alone with him. As long as I fed him regularly, he didn't even sniff in her direction. So she read to him, brought him yarn, tempted him with smoothies (which he disdained), and in general found him fascinating. He was keeping clean, too, and showering on his own. I'd borrowed lots of clothes for him from Marc and Eric, though he refused socks and underpants. He took the yarn she offered, slipped off the paper covering, and started to roll it into a ball.

I finished Noxema-ing my face—I might be eternally young, but vampires got dirty faces just like everyone else. Those little disposable towelettes were a godsend; I kept a ton in my purse. "I guess we'll have to keep an eye on her."

"You didn't figure that out after the mysterious weapons of hellfire?"

"Yeah, but now I *really* want to keep an eye on her. I mean, it's great that she turned her back on her destiny—"

"But can you really?" Jessica asked quietly.

"Exactly. I mean, look at Eric and me. I swore we'd never be together, but—"

"Your inner whore would not be denied," she finished.

"That is *not* what I was going to say."

"Sure," she sneered.

"You know, you could go back to not talking to me again."

"You wish."

Two hours later, I was just getting to the part in the movie where Rhett sweeps a struggling Scarlett up the stairs when the phone at my elbow rang. Oooh, Clark Gable! I was normally not a fan of facial hair, but he was the exception to the rule. Those lips, those eyes! And the phone was still ringing. Nuts. I had to do everything myself.

I picked it up, gaze still riveted to the screen. "Hello?"

"Good evening, Your Majesty. I hope you don't mind my calling instead of seeing you in person, but there's so much to do, I'm a little short on time."

"Who the hell is this?"

"It's Andrea," she said, sounding worried.

"Oh, right. That was a test, Andrea. And you just passed."

"Thank you, Your Majesty. I was just calling to make sure you had everything you needed for tomorrow night."

"Tomorrow night?"

"My wedding," Andrea prompted me thinly.

"Oh. Oh! Right! Your wedding. I totally didn't forget about it again. Wow, tomorrow's Halloween already, huh?"

"No. Tomorrow is the rehearsal."

"Right, right. Well, I guess we'll see you tomorrow."

"My father can't make it, and my mother is out of the country . . ." She trailed off. I happened to know (from Tina, who was a remarkably tactful but accurate gossip) that Andrea's parents thought she was still dead. Well, none of my business.

"Hey," I said suddenly. "Do you mind if my sister comes?" Laura would get a kick out of it, not to mention Operation Keep an Eye on the Spawn of Satan would be a lot easier. And if there was a sudden wedding coup, she'd come in handy. "It's up to you, it's your wedding, but—"

"Your—no, of course not. I'd be honored. Any of your family members are welcome."

"That's nice of you, but I put my foot down with my mom."

"Ma'am, that's not necessary."

"No, it totally is. She's looking at this from a cultural perspective, and I can just tell she's dying to corner Tina and grill her about Life Back Then."

"Truly, Your Majesty. I don't mind." Andrea sounded like she was cheering up. "Someone's mother should be there."

"Oh." When you put it that way. "Well, okay. I'll let her know. She'll be thrilled. Sincerely."

"That sounds wonderful." Yep, she had definitely cheered

up. I felt a little better. It was bad enough that my dad knew I was dead and ignored me. What must it be like for her?

For that matter, what must it be like to outlive your whole family? Not that it was Andrea's problem yet, but it would be. It was Tina's and Sinclair's right now, and had been for years. Someday it would be mine. Mom, Dad, the Ant, Jessica, Marc . . . all gone. Laura, too? I didn't know. With her fiendish powers and low cholesterol, she could live for five hundred years.

I shook it off. "So we'll see you tomorrow, then. Say hi to Daniel for me."

"I will. Good night, Majesty."

I hung up and hit the Stop button on the DVD player. Yikes! The wedding! Time to go shopping before I forgot about it again.

Chapter 33

Satan appeared to me while I was sipping a medium Orange Julius and flipping through that month's *Real Simple.* There was a small sitting area near the Orange Julius stand (technically, it was Cinnabon's property) and I was relaxing and pondering where to go next—Nordstrom or GapBaby.

I'd found a black cashmere dress to go with my purple pumps, but I was still watching out for the perfect accessory. And there was the gestating baby to consider; it wasn't a minute too soon to try to counteract the Ant's tacky taste.

Suddenly, there she was, sitting across from me. The devil. Satan. The lord of lies. And it wasn't any big shock—I'd known it would be coming. And I instantly knew who she was. Some things you just know, the way you just know you shouldn't wear true black mascara because it makes your eyes look small and squinty.

The devil, in case you ever wanted to know, is a woman in her late forties. Today, she was wearing a dark gray suit that buttoned up the front and looked almost military, black panty hose, and plain black pumps. Her hair was a rich chocolate brown, with steaks of silver at the temples, and done up in an elegant bun. Her eyes were very black. Her ears weren't pierced; in fact, the devil wore no jewelry at all.

She studied me from across the table for a few moments. Finally she said, "You are the vampire queen."

It wasn't a question, so I guessed she wasn't taking a poll. I wiped my mouth. "Uh . . . yeah."

"Elizabeth Taylor."

"Yes." From pure force of habit, I checked out her shoes again . . . then looked one more time. What I had first taken for plain black pumps were in fact Roger Vivier comma heels. Vivier customized footwear for celebrities; his shoes were literally one of a kind. Queen Elizabeth had worn a pair to her coronation. I was looking at hand-tooled shoes with garnets in the heels.

Circa 1962. Only sixteen pairs were made.

They were the holy grail of footgear.

"Wh—where did you get those?"

The devil gave me a wintry smile. "Would you like them?"

Yes! No. Would I sell my soul for shoes? Of course not. The very idea was absurd. And the gleam of the garnets didn't call to me, the very idea of selling my teeny little soul wasn't a bargain at any . . . no!

"And you are half sibling to my daughter, Favored of the Morning Star?"

"What? Oh, you mean Laura? Right, that's what the Book called her. I guess 'Spawn of Satan' didn't have as nice a ring to it."

The devil had a superb poker face. "The Book. You shouldn't have tried to destroy it."

Tried to? One thing at a time. "Yeah, well, it didn't go with anything else in the library."

"That sort of thing could be considered blasphemy. Consider the average Catholic's reaction if the Pope threw a first-edition Bible into the Mississippi River. Now consider the message you just sent to your servants."

"They aren't my servants."

"Wait."

"Look, can we get back on topic? You were asking about Laura? Thanks *so* much for helping us at Scratch, by the way."

"I'm more of a watcher than a doer," Satan admitted. "Besides, I knew the two of you would prevail. In fact, the two of you combined are virtually unstoppable. Virtually."

"Yeha, yeah."

This was the devil. *The* devil! The worst creature in the whole universe. The reason people killed their husbands and ran over little kids in the road and drank too much and did drugs and raped and murdered and lied and cheated and stole. So I admit I was a bit cautious, even if the devil did look weirdly like Lena Olin.

"He still loves you, you know."

"Yep, I sure do know."

"In case you were having doubts. It seems to me that it's been a rough couple of weeks for you, so I'll set you straight on that, at least: He will always love you."

"Yes, I know."

(Later, Jessica would ask me, "Who was she talking about?" and I would tell her, "God. She was talking about God." This weirded out the vampires, but Jess thought it was very fine. As for me, I'd always known the truth. Yeah, it had been a bad couple of weeks, but I'd never doubted *that*.)

She sniffed. "It's too bad. My daughter has the same problem. You could have been formidable. *She* still will be."

"I wouldn't bet the farm on that one."

"I love to bet." She studied me, her blue eyes narrowing. Er, hadn't they been brown a minute ago? "Definitely a shame. You might have been someone to contend with. You still could be, if you jettison a few silly ideas."

"Oh, I don't mind," I assured the devil. "That was never, you know, a career goal or anything."

"Humph." The devil narrowed her hazel eyes. "Your stepmother was the perfect vessel for me."

"Oh, I'm sure," I said truthfully.

"And your father is a fool."

Okay, now I was starting to get a little annoyed. What'd I ever do to the devil? Besides not be completely and foully evil all the time? And not sell my soul for her shoes? Which I hadn't entirely ruled out yet. "Are we going to talk about anything I haven't figured out for myself? Because I was sort of hoping this would be an interesting conversation. I mean, you *do* have a reputation."

The devil smirked. "Wretched child."

"Look, it's kind of weirding me out to be talking to you here."

"I have been here many times."

"Ooooh, wow, a commentary on our grasping culture and how the mall culture is secretly the root of all evil! I'd never pick up on *that*. I've seen freight trains that were more subtle."

The devil glared. "I was just making an observation."

"Yeah, well, make another one."

"You're one step up from being a moron."

"I'm rubber and you're glue," I told Satan, "and everything that bounces off me sticks to you."

She narrowed her green eyes and looked like she might come over the table at me. After a long moment, she said, "Look after my Laura, if you please."

"Well, sure."

"I have big plans for her."

"Okay. That's not humongously creepy or anything."

She crossed her leg and pointed her toe up, giving me a look at the sole of her shoe. Totally unmarked. Oh, God. They were in perfect shape.

"Last chance," the devil said.

"Get thee behind me, Lena Olin."

She disappeared in a puff of smoke that smelled like rotten eggs. No, really. She did. And I went back to *Real Simple*. It was either that or have hysterics in the food court, and I did have some pride left.

Chapter 34

Exhausted from shopping and my Orange Julius with Satan, I staggered into my room and saw the large box sitting on the end of my bed. It was a plain brown cardboard box, so I honestly didn't think anything of it. It was boot-sized, so I figured Jess had picked me up a pair of winter boots to kick around in while she was out and about.

I flipped off the top of the box . . . and nearly fell *into* the box. There, nestled in crisp white tissue paper, were Kate Spade's Mondrian boots, way out of my reach at five hundred bucks. A dream in buttery black and red leather, with an inch and a half heel, they looked sleek and cool just sitting there. I could practically hear them telling me "Vrooom, vrooom!"

"Oooh, oooh," I gurgled, totally beyond coherent speech. *Me likey!* I snatched them up—tissue paper and box and all—to my chest. "Ooooh!"

Instantly rejuvenated, I whipped around to dart out and show them to—well, anybody—and there was Sinclair standing in the doorway, smiling. His dark eyes sparkled and he said, "Since you seduced me, it seemed only fair that I seduce you."

"Oh, baby!" I cried, and danced across the room to give him a kiss.

Chapter 35

"Okay, so, to finish up . . ." I glanced back down at my notes. This wasn't as hard as I'd thought it was going to be; there weren't very many people there to worry about (which was both good and bad) and, frankly, I looked great. So did the bride, in a cream-colored sheath and a set of grayish pearls, bareheaded, with flawless makeup. Daniel was in a dark suit of some kind, but who cared? Weddings weren't about the groom.

Daniel hadn't told his dad (for obvious reasons, but still, it was sad), planning to later explain his "elopement" with the new Mrs. Daniels, who had a horror of sunlight. Andrea's family wasn't there. My mom and my sister were, as were Marc and Jessica, Sinclair and Tina. George was enchanted with his new #6 crochet needle, and refused to come out of the basement.

So I wasn't especially nervous, but I wanted it to be nice. "I did some research on nondenominational weddings . . . obviously nondenominational . . . and I found this on the Web. Okay, it goes like this.

" 'May the promises you make to one another be lived out to the end of your lives in an atmosphere of profoundest joy.' " I paused. Daniel and Andrea were positively google-eyed at each other, and Mom was sniffling like she always does at weddings.

All part of my diabolical plan, so I went on. "I thought that would be good advice for anybody, regardless of special, uh, circumstances. So now we'll do the vows, and then we'll have punch. Do you, Daniel, choose to marry Andrea? To speak words that will join you with her as your wife for all the rest of the days of your life?"

"I will."

"Do you, Andrea, choose to marry Daniel? To speak words that will join you with him as your husband for all the rest of the days of your life?"

I paused again. That was the big question. Andrea had a long, long life ahead of her. And Daniel was no sheep. How would they make this work? Would she try to turn him into a vampire? Would he allow it?

It was none of my business. Better to focus on the day and worry about that stuff later.

"I will."

"Then by the power invested in me, by me, I now pronounce you husband and wife. Bite away."

They ignored me and kissed, but that was all right.

"I have one more thing," I said. "From Shakespeare. Don't look so surprised, my search engine works. Anyway, as soon as I saw it I thought of you two, so I figured this would be a good place to mention it." I didn't mention it was from *Romeo and Juliet*; hopefully their romance would turn out better.

> *"With love's light wings did I o'erperch these walls,*
> *For stony limits cannot hold love out,*
> *And what love can do, that dares love attempt."*

I finished and looked up from my notes.

From across the room, Sinclair was smiling at me.